Strange Magic

Mark Hammar

Gray Wolf Publishing
WWW.GRAYWOLFPUB.BIZLAND.COM
graywolfpub@yahoo.com

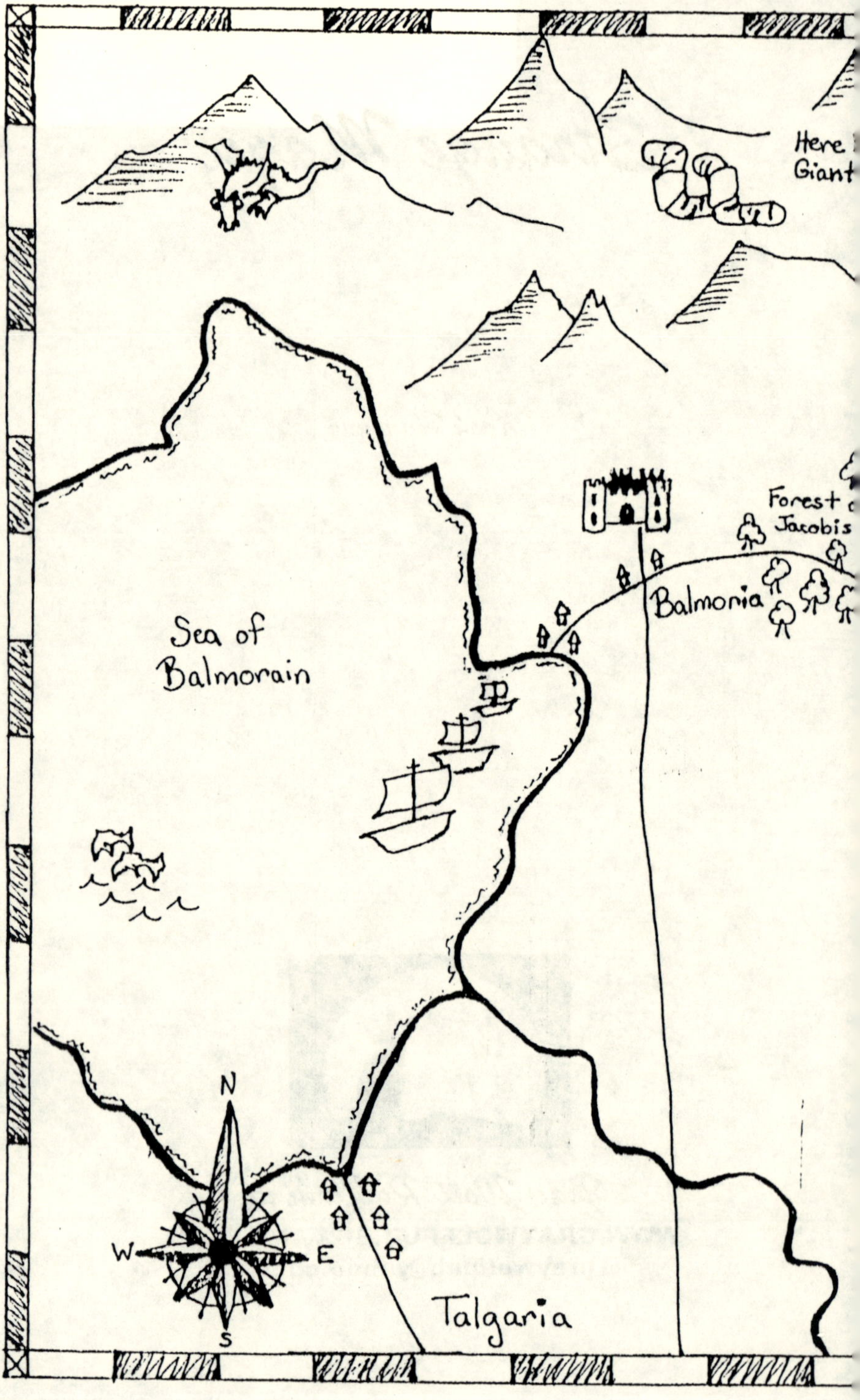
Here
Giant
Forest
Jacobis
Balmoria
Sea of
Balmorain
N
W
E
S
Talgaria

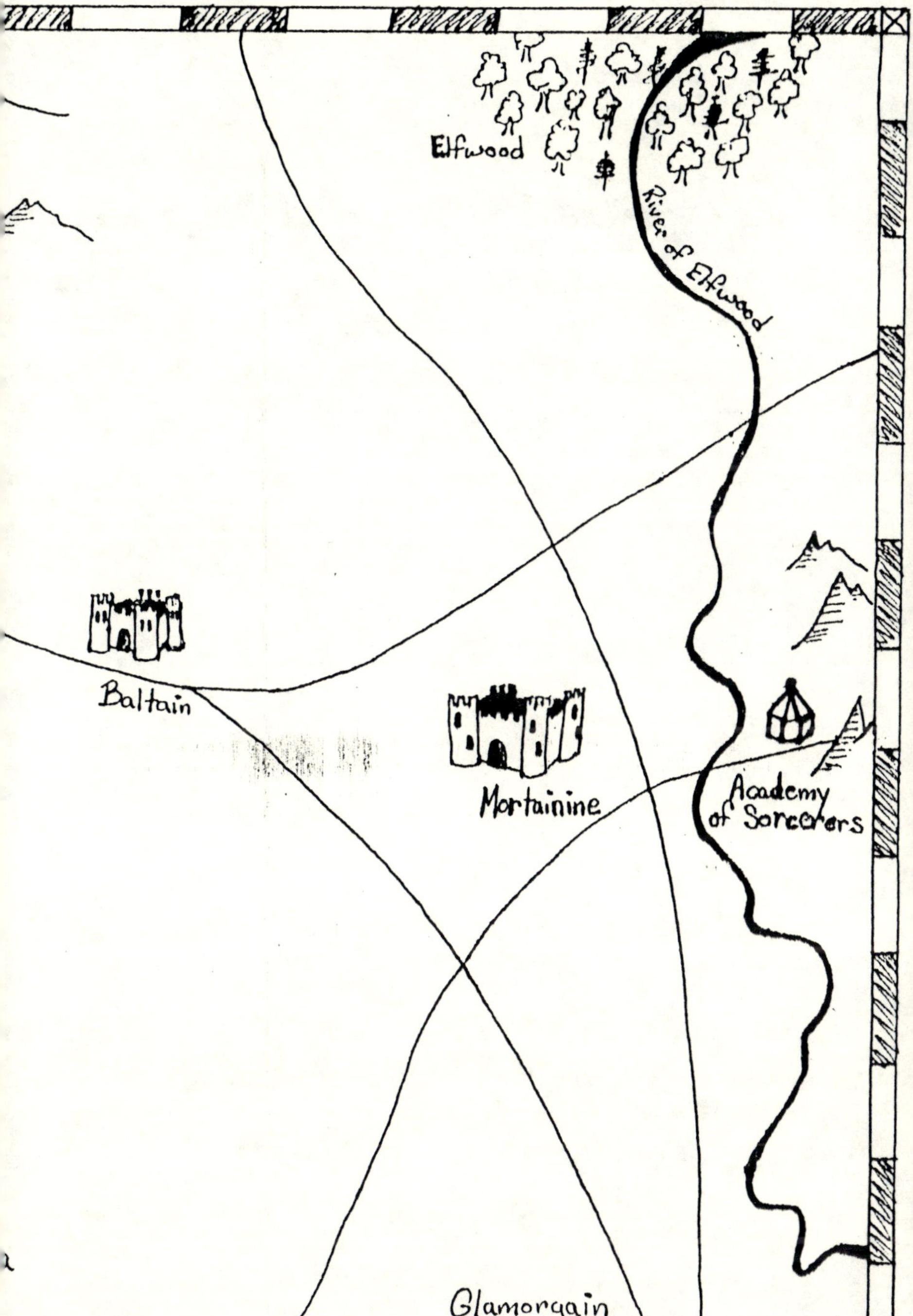
Elfwood
River of Elfwood
Baltain
Mortainine
Academy of Sorcerers
Glamorgain

To Grica,

Thanks for many years of friendship.

Mark Hamman
Gilwell '91

First Gray Wolf Publishing Edition, 2000

Published in Canada by Gray Wolf Publishing in 2000.

WWW.GRAYWOLFPUB.BIZLAND.COM
graywolfpub@yahoo.com

Hammar, Mark, 1967 -
For storytelling: mark_hammar@yahoo.com

Strange Magic

Martha Lynn Lawson
Cover Art and Internal Art

ISBN 0-9686136-0-8

Printed and Bound in Canada

Dedicated to my wife without whose support and encouragement I would not have finished this book. Also to my mentor Bill Evans, and to the cubs I have had the pleasure to lead over the years, because they both inspired me to tell stories.

0
Young Princeling

Justin was four when he learned the way of things. Life was laid out for him and his siblings as neatly as a pattern on a tapestry, as it had been for generations in his family. His oldest sister Jeanetta, the first child of King Charlie, was to dedicate her life to rule and would secede the King when he died. She was to learn the arts of war and diplomacy so that she could one day sit on the throne of Balmoria and conduct wise and honest dealings with the neighbouring countries. Through the king's tutoring she would continue the long and prosperous history of the small northern country, and bring up her children in their rightful place.

His older brother Peter, the second child of the King, was to learn from his Aunt Rebekah the life of a Cleric and the ways of the gods. He was to become a runecaster and reader of the oracles under the guidance of his aunt. From her he would learn all there was to know about tracking the Solar festivals, and the lunar calendar. He would learn to use the power of the trees to cure and prevent disease, and to divine an image of the future from the rune stones or Ogham sticks.

Justin himself, the third and last child of the King, was to learn from his Uncle Arthur the practice of magic and the manner of the Sorcerer. To learn the arts required to protect the country from all manner of magic and mystery when the time came for him to take the position of court sorcerer. As foretold in prophecy each generation of the monarchy would have three children and they would dedicate their lives to these disciplines. So, at the tender age of four and a half, Justin went to spend most of his life with his Uncle in the tower.

Justin spent many hours studying the laws of nature as apprentice to his uncle, the court sorcerer. He learned how the trees intermingled with the birds, how the birds visited the flowers, and how the flowers carpeted the grass beneath the trees. Uncle Arthur would take his apprentice up into the tower for days at a time, filling the court and peasants with awe at the thought of their seclusion. Then, after an hour of setting small fires burning under bowls of foul smelling liquids and setting smoke puffs to be released every hour, Arthur and Justin would don simple garments and creep down a hidden back stairway to spend days in the woods, living off the land and their wits, eating only what nature or a humble farmer or wood cutter supplied. For a young boy this deception provided endless fun and excitement.

Justin was almost eight when he first questioned his Uncle about his education. He had learned a lot about how nature worked, and how to change nature through experiment, but he felt an empty something in his learning. Something was missing, something was wrong. His Uncle took him to the top of a nearby mountain and sat him on a rock.

"My dear nephew. I have waited so long for you to ask just this question, and I will answer it thus. This mountain on which we stand, how is it measured in importance?" Justin stared and thought a long time, his Uncle waiting patiently.

"By its size, I suppose, my Uncle."

"And how did it attain this importance, where did it learn?" The question puzzled Justin.

"Learn to be a mountain? It just, IS, a mountain I guess." Justin hazarded an answer. His Uncle answered the unasked question. *'What do you mean?'*

"A Sorcerers magic," he said, "is like the mountain in two ways. It cannot be learned, it merely is. One cannot learn to be magic, one can only use magic like one uses the mountain. This is the first way in which magic is like a mountain. The other way is that, like a mountain, magic draws its importance from the perception of others, it is not important in and of itself. Magic is in everything, and around everything, and through everything, yet it is nothing. Do you not understand my child?" Arthur stood over Justin and awaited his answer.

"I think that I do not my Uncle," answered Justin. Arthur nodded his head.

"Your eighth birth celebration is upon you. The time has indeed come. To the east lies a larger mountain than this, and at its base stands a building of learning. A building of Sorcerers. In this building you will be taught all that you need to know about the magic of sorcery and the ways of working nature. After nine years you will return, my worthy apprentice. Show them this at the door and they will let you enter." He placed an amulet around Justin's neck, on it was the sign of a hawk. "Come now, we must return." Justin felt the amulet around his neck with his fingers, then he turned and followed his uncle.

That night he was startled from a deep sleep by his Uncle gently shaking his shoulder. He woke with a start. The Sorcerers gentle voice calmed him at once. "My child, remember this one thing. Magic is five parts what you do and ninety-five parts what others think you did. Sorcery is science, witchcraft is true magic. Sleep now." When Justin woke this was only a faint memory in his mind.

In the next few months Justin's birth celebration arrived and the time for his departure drew near. In the spring of his eighth year, the caravan from the southwest made its yearly journey through Balmoria on its way east to the trading centres in Mortainine. Its arrival always brought joy and feasting as the people of Balmoria traded with the caravan during the day and listened to news and stories from afar around the fire at night. After a late night of stories and food around the castle fire, Justin packed his few belongings for the trip to the School of Sorcerers, a days journey past Mortainine. When the morning came, and the caravan struck camp and moved on, Justin was ready to join them on their trek.

In the company of this caravan traveled a storyteller named Bard, who fast became friends with the young sorcerer. Justin liked him as much for his friendly and confident manner, as for the tales he could tell as they traveled. Five days into the journey they emerged on the eastern side of the Forest of Jacobis and he could see the top of the mountain, which his Uncle had told him about, on the very distant horizon. Bard told of the many men and women who had gone before Justin into the academy of learning. Six days later, as they entered the town of Baltain for a much needed stop and rest, the mountain was still in the far distance. They stayed in Baltain for two days as they traded goods and news much like they had in Balmoria. Justin was in awe over his first visit to the sister castle of Balmoria, and the days passed quickly as he searched every nook and cranny of the town to see what there was to see. They set out in the morning after their third night and

Justin's mind was once again on the mountain in the distance, and the Academy of Sorcerers.

After another sixteen days, as the caravan came to the trading centers in Mortainine, the mountain finally drew near. After a day in the trading center, Bard accompanied Justin on the last day of his trip. With his friend he had come through storms and long hours of walking over the hills and vales of the land, now they had crossed over the last river which ran from the Elfwood in the north and past the academy. They were standing at the door to the great institute of sorcery, and the time had come for Justin to say goodbye. Bard shook his hand with a promise to be there to meet him for his return at the end of his schooling, then turned and walked away. Justin turned and used the large, heavy knocker on the door.

A tall, robed man opened the door and asked his business. Justin silently handed over the amulet Arthur had given him and followed at the tall man's gesture. They entered a great hall, along the walls of which hung dozens of amulets like the one Justin had until recently carried. Each amulet had a different symbol emblazoned on the crest. Falcons, crows and eagles. Wolves, foxes and weasels. Dragons, Nymphs and Satyrs. Every manner of beast known and imagined. Justin was to learn that each amulet belonged to a sorcerer who either had an apprentice at the school or had died. The sorcerer walked to one of many spots on the wall, which was empty save for a peg. Under this peg was written the name *'ARTHUR'* in bold script. The man hung the amulet on the peg and escorted Justin to the room that he was to call home for the next nine years. The door closed behind him, and all was silent.

1
Return

A tall lone figure glided down the road towards the stark, quiet castle. He was enshrouded in a long, dark grey robe. On his feet were strapped sturdy sandals, and over his shoulder hung a satchel. The right hand firmly held a long, crooked staff. Slowly the figure drifted along the quiet road as the first light of day was breaking the crest of the earth behind. For a brief moment the shape stopped and surveyed the land it remembered, as if from a dream. The wandering son had returned.

No news had reached him through the last dozen years, the institute was completely blocked from the outside world, all his time had been spent in his studies. He knew nothing of the affairs of Balmoria until after his graduation, on the feast of Beltane, when he had met with Bard again for the return trip home. Bard had taken him aside before the trip began, sat him down, and told him the history of this kingdom of his youth. The shock of his father and oldest sister's death made him seclude himself in a room for three days before he was ready to go into the world. After this time alone, and the long trip home, he had thought he was ready for what awaited him. He was wrong.

The farmers' fields lay barren and wasted, and the lands of forested hills and vales had been cut or burnt to the ground leaving miles of stark, open space as far as the eye could see. Where towering forests had once stood, bare infertile desert yielded only small stalks of withered grass and dust weeds. To the west he could see the top of the solitary mast belonging to the Kingdom's lone sailing ship, which lay scuttled in the harbour. Justin slowly restarted his trek across the destitute void between him and the once mighty castle still towering on the small hill.

The town, which had once surrounded the castle, thriving and growing, now stood in burnt ruins. The magician paced quietly through the abandoned streets of the town, raising no dust as he lifted and set his feet upon the earthen pathways. The desolate buildings around him made his heart sink. Coming to the trail that lead to the sturdy front doors of his childhood home brought tears to his eyes.

The once mighty oaks and elms that had stood guarding the long path to the castle gate had been felled and, judging from the markings on the door, used as battering rams on the castle. The gates of the castle had been badly beaten and worn since his leaving, the turrets were damaged and in need of repair. The portcullis was a rusted, twisted mesh of metal, yet it held. In the doorway, despite the unspeakable horror of the world around them, stood two welcome, friendly faces, awaiting his arrival.

***

Uncle Arthur and Aunt Rebekah met Justin at the Portcullis, their faces, though friendly, were set in the most painful look of depression and sorrow. Arthur, with his silvered hair and careworn face, stood as tall as Justin, some two and a half armlengths tall. Rebekah, her hair still blond but her face equally care worn, stood slightly shorter than the two sorcerers. Justin greeted them warmly, banishing his tears, and was escorted into the castle. In the center of the courtyard stood a large, pensive looking, Saguaro cactus, an oddity in the cold climate of the kingdom. Around this plant were small tents, which housed the remaining families of the town who had not been killed or chased out. Uncle Arthur spoke first.

"How good to see you my lad. We feared you would not make it past the siege. What news from the Academy of Sorcerers?" Justin took the hawk amulet from around his neck where it hung next to his own, emblazoned with an owl. This he handed back to his Uncle, who took it gladly.

"The academy fairs better than Balmoria. The death of Father and Jeanetta is surely a tragedy felt by all. How fairs Peter in his new role as King?" As Justin spoke they slowly walked across the courtyard.

"He stands there, ruling no farther that he can move." Aunt Rebekah pointed at the cactus as she spoke. "He seems not to fair very well even though we feed and water him every day. Such a plant I have never seen before. The people need you to rule in his place now." The cactus did indeed look forlorn, ragged and morose as Rebekah spoke of him. Justin looked quickly, then walked on in quiet contemplation. At the entrance to the castle proper he stopped.

"We must meet immediately in my father's war room. Please assemble everyone necessary there in one hour." Justin nodded his thanks and turned to enter. He stopped and faced his Aunt and Uncle once again. "And we should cut Peter's watering to once every month. And have someone build a shelter around him and warm it with a fire. He should do much better after that." He turned and once again started the walk back to the room he used to occupy as a child.

***

Justin's room looked just as he had left it, except that everything was covered in a thick layer of dust. In the far east corner stood a high bookshelf beside a sturdy wooden bed. Justin dropped his bag unceremoniously beside the open door, walked to the shelf, and took down a large leather bound book from the top row. The book was titled 'Cities of the South', and when opened looked like any ordinary book. Justin had modified it himself and, after turning a dozen pages, the leaves refused to turn. They had been glued and the center cut from the leaves to form a secure hiding place for some of his most treasured memories of childhood. Opening it now brought back thoughts and feelings, which had been buried in the back of his mind for over a decade. The small sheathed knife he had used as a youngster to help his Uncle cut and collect herbs and plants for their spells and potions. A dried, pressed flower given to him by his best childhood friend, Lynette. Numerous baubles and bangles which each held a special place in his heart and mind, a place where these troubles could not touch them. He returned the collection, closed the book, and returned it to its shelf. These riches would have to wait for a later day.

Justin cleared away some of the clutter from the room and placed his sparse collection of clothing into their required places. He removed his sandals and lay down on the bed, unaware of how weary his trip had made him. He slept soundly before waking to the timer in his head. The time had come to meet with his country's protectors.

***

Justin surveyed the room of chairs, nearly all of which were empty. His childhood friend Lynette, who was sitting at the far end of the table, threw a friendly, almost wistful, smile at him. Two young girls sat quietly in the corner of the room, not daring to utter a word. Many of the places around the table were left vacant, only to be explained by the tale his Aunt was soon to unfold. One chair, that of the chief strategist, sat hauntingly empty. Rebekah started to update him on the events of the past years he had missed while away.

The witch had emerged from a cave in the mountains to the north some two years earlier, the same mountains which Justin had climbed as a child, nearly ten years before. At first she was only heard of through rumour and conjecture, but then she started to make her presence known. Seven months after she had moved into the neighbourhood the witch, Deirdre by name, had sent a message down to the castle demanding an audience with the King. It was the feast of Samhain. King Charlie accepted this meeting and had heard the woman out. After an hour long meeting the witch had stormed out of the hall and through the castle gates, returning to the mountains. Charlie had sat sullenly in his chambers for hours before emerging to explain the outcome to his advisors. She had demanded half of the kingdom from the north mountains, across to the eastern woods and to the western sea harbour. Along with this she had demanded a yearly tribute of half the treasury. The King had refused. Deirdre had explained her predictions of the outcome for the Kings family, and had not let him reconsider. This was the point at which she had stormed out. The King never expanded on her predictions, but judging by his mood they had been explicit and far from pleasant. That night, during the festival to welcome the dark half of the year, the Ice Wyrms had come into the village.

At this Justin started. Ice Wyrms were longer than three men and were as big around as a small hut.

Everyone knew that they lived in the northeastern corner of the mountains, but nowhere in recorded history had they ever strayed this far from their lairs. The biggest threat from the Wyrms had come from young boys and girls who had thought they would show their courage by seeking their lairs. Of these some had returned with badly frozen bits, and some had not returned at all. These stories had been enough to keep the populace away and in the recent past no incidents had been noted. But to have the Ice Wyrms come to the village was unheard of.

The Ice Wyrms had caused a panic in the small village surrounding the castle. A scarce twenty-four people were killed in the bedlam, but the majority were frightened half to their deaths. The castle guard had been alerted and had managed to route the Wyrms, but it was evident that this only happened because the Wyrms were unused to resistance. When they learned to cope with it they would be a formidable enemy. The King called a council of his people. He explained the witch's threat, and the witch's tactics. He then urged all those who wished, to move to safer realms. Few had done this, most had stayed. After a few recurring nights of Ice Wyrm attacks, spaced over some weeks, the remaining villagers crowded into the confines of the Castle courtyard. Then all fell silent until just before the feast of Yule, when the winds of winter blew over the land.

The calm ended with a loud rumble. It was the sound of many tiny bodies being forced into larger ones. Throughout the kingdom, every mouse and rat was being turned. Each grew to a six foot stance, broad shouldered and strong. Their humanoid bodies, though still covered in fur, were the size of the strongest soldier and each was topped with a large rodent head, with teeth as sharp as knives. The castle soldiers had barely expelled the rodents from the gates before they had overrun the castle.

In a few weeks the mighty army of rodents was armed by the witch and amassed to attack the castle. The King, more annoyed than frightened by the rodents, gathered his castle army and led the defense. That first battle had proven to be worse than the King had expected. The strengthened rodents had beaten the army into retreat, pursuing them even to the castle gates where they were beaten off by pots of boiling oil and archers. One soldier for every ten who fought in the battle died. This did not bode well for a small army, with no recruiting capabilities, fighting an untrained enemy. By comparison the witch's forces were great in number and could be easily replenished. It was in this battle that Jeanetta had met her demise. Having learned only few of the skills of a war leader and even less of a warrior, she and her charger Baltain had been easy fodder for the rodents' swords when they had broken as far as the rear lines of the army.

The story continued to unfold as Justin listened. The continued rodent attacks, followed by more Ice Wyrm assaults, soon took their toll on the army, which grew weary with the constant aggressions. These attacks lasted for over a year, until the great blow had happened just before the last feast of Imbolc, only four months prior to Justin's return. King Charlie had fallen in battle. The new King, Peter, was ordained within the week, and lit the funeral pier of the late King as his first royal act. The ashes of the blaze were not even cold when Peter stood in the courtyard to announce his continued resistance against the witch and her army. As his words echoed around the castle walls the cheers of the crowd fell silent. With a puff of green smoke, the form of the new King was replaced with a large, green, spined plant, its arms stretched towards the sky as Peter's had been during his announcement.

After this tragedy Rebekah searched frantically to find an answer as to why this had happened. Peter, as all clerics, possessed a holy talisman to ward off evil and protect him from spells. In searching his belongings, Rebekah could find no trace of this coveted holy symbol. She could only guess that Peter had lost his amulet while blessing the dead and dying on the battleground, and that the witch had found it and held it to cast her spell over the young King when the time was presented.

The tale drew to a close and Justin again scanned the faces of the small, expectant group, five in number. Along with his Aunt and Uncle sat Lynette, the last remaining troop commander, and two silent young girls. He waited for a few long moments before he spoke. "I must be by myself for a few hours to take stock of the situation. Please excuse me, I will address the people when I return." He rose and, nodding to his Uncle, slowly left the room.

***

As in the past, his Uncle met him at the entrance to the castle tower. They entered the familiar stairwell and slowly climbed the circular staircase together. At length Justin spoke.

"Not everything was revealed at the meeting, Uncle, for instance who were the two young girls seated in the far chairs. And what of Malcolm, father's personal aid and greatest strategist? He could always defeat me at the simulated battles we played."

"The young girls are your sisters, Shanawn and Megan. They were conceived shortly after your departure and born within a year of your leaving. At birth they were nearly identical, yet now they are as different as night from day. Megan, the one with blond hair and blue eyes, is a silent yet brilliant girl. As good a student as yourself. Shanawn is the one with the darker hair and the eyes of hazel. She is more outgoing, yet equally intelligent, and is constantly being silenced by your Aunt for something she has said. The people pay them little heed though, being fourths, and twins as well. That is just not done. The people take it as a sign and evil omen, yet they fear to react against them since they are from the royal family. A good thing from my point of view. So they sit and wait, only talking and learning when we have opportunity. Which is seldom of late."

"What of mother, where has she gone?" Justin feared the answer.

"Another reason for the people to cast dispersion on the twins. Your mother died giving birth to the two girls. She was so loved by your father and the people. If this threat had come sooner I do not know how he would have fared. As it was he did not fight like he had in the past, partly due to his age, but I suspect partly from grief as well."

"As to Malcolm he was felled in the first battle. Although he was not killed, his voice box was cut and damaged. I fear he can never talk again. The other soldiers have unknowingly shunned him in spite of themselves, though kindly. He can no longer lead as he once did. The only person that I can think would understand him now is your aunt, Rebekah."

"And what does she know that no one else does?"

"When Malcolm was a young man he came to join the kings army at the age of thirteen years, since his parents had died from a disease and he had no means of sustaining himself. Your aunt was only twelve years of age herself, and the two became close friends. For the next three years the two were never seen apart during their free hours, and I dare say that they should have been married if their positions were any different. However at that time a cleric did not marry a soldier, and if there is one thing that your aunt does unfailingly it is to stick to ritual. So, because of this, they remained only as friends. Malcolm was a brilliant soldier and had quickly become a commander, and the duties of a cleric were taking more time from the young couple. Soon they had little time to talk, and even less alone. That was when they developed it."

"Developed what, Uncle Arthur?"

"They developed a way of talking with their hands. They thought no one knew, but I figured out their game. They would make hand signals to each other across the table in the war room, or in the courtyard when the troops were gathered for practice. They were very good and could talk fluently after a time, although I could never understand what they were saying. I have never told anyone about this until today, and I have not seen them use this speech as of late. I wonder if they would still remember how to do it?" As Arthur finished his tale the two turned the corner at the top of the stairs. Standing in the center of the room in front of them, larger than life, were two humanoid rats. Justin immediately drew his sword in defense.

"They have overrun the castle. Quickly Uncle, call for help." Arthur's hand rested swiftly on his shoulder, holding his hand.

"Return your sword, Justin, they are friends. These are the rats I kept in the lab when you were a lad. I managed to turn the witch's spell to avoid the change in their brains to evil and obedience to her. No one else knows of their existence. Matthew, Mortimer, do you remember Justin my apprentice?" The two Giant rodents nodded and held out their hands in friendship. Justin re-sheathed his sword and took their offered hands.

"And how did you manage to hold them Uncle, when the witches powers had already begun to change them." Justin noted the large muscles of the rodents, and the agility with which they walked.

"I merely placed a metal bucket over their heads, reflecting the magic from their brains. The reflection did however create something of an unexpected result. This is Sally, Justin. Sally this is Justin." Justin followed his Uncles directing finger toward a human size, black spider walking in his direction. "It appears that the deflected magic could not turn a spiders mind."

"We spiders have very strong wills." Sally added sweetly, with a voice that could entice a fly into a web.

Justin fell heavily into a chair, his head spinning with this new knowledge. Malcolm muted, a new set of sisters, two mice and a spider on the side of his army. At length he stood. "Matthew, Mortimer, Sally. Come with me." Then turning to Arthur, "I will address the people." He turned to the stairs and saw Megan and Shanawn standing at the top. He embraced them warmly. "You shall come also, my sisters. Our people await our greeting." They walked slowly down the stairs.

2
Preparations for Battle

Justin stood on the castle wall overlooking the courtyard. To his left stood Matthew, Mortimer and Sally. To his right stood Arthur, Rebekah, and the newly found Malcolm who stood with a red cloak wrapped around his torso and a shock of silver hair adorning his nearly bald head. Shanawn and Megan stood to the right as well. Justin addressed the people who stood in awe to see him standing in the company of the unspoken and the enemy. Justin held his hands high to silence the murmuring of the crowd.

"My friends, my people, I stand before you with those who are considered our foes and those who are seldom spoken of. I do so because they, as well as yourselves, will be our salvation. Matthew and Mortimer, along with Sally, were created by the witch but held from turning evil by our Court Sorcerer, Arthur." The three animals stood quietly as Justin spoke. "They will give us an insight into the minds of the animals who attack us, as well as two fighter who are as strong as our opponents." Many in the crowd murmured skeptically as the three animals stood in silence.

"Malcolm, though dispossessed of his voice, is still in possession of his superior abilities to plan a battle. He and our Cleric Rebekah will learn to talk to each other through the use of hand gestures so that we will be able to use his superior tactical abilities." The Soldier and Cleric gazed at Justin with a questioning look. He smiled and nodded to Arthur, who winked at them with a certain mischievous pleasure in his eyes. The two knew that their secret had been discovered.

"Also Megan and Shanawn will need to take my place as Sorcerers Apprentice's with the sudden demise of Jeanetta. They have already been learning from Arthur and have proven to be good students in his craft." The crowd, though uncertain and suspicious, could not help but admit to this fact. If Balmoria were to continue as it had, there needed to be a magician, or magicians, to take Arthur's place.

"Lastly, all citizens must present themselves for war duty. The young who can fight will be trained to do so. Those who can pull a bow will practice in its use. The others will support by learning fletching, smithing, and baking for the battle forces. All can make themselves useful and that is what we will need to defeat the witch's forces. The witch thinks we are a depleted army, but we will raise a new army before her eyes. Are all with me?"

The crowd, though still uncertain about the animals and the twins, cheered their approval for Justin. Though they may question some of his methods, their only chance was with Justin and his menagerie of leaders. Arthur rose to his feet. "Because your brother is not dead, you cannot be crowned King. However, we are empowering you with the circlet crown of the warrior King to be worn in your brother's place until he can be restored to us." He walked over to the young prince and, drawing the crown from a fold in his cloak, placed it on the head of Justin, the Sorcerer King. The crowd's cheers rose higher as their hopes began to soar. Even the large saguaro in the courtyard seemed to beam with joy.

***

Within hours new recruits were being trained in the art of swordplay and archery, while others were learning to make arrows, swords and other supplies needed by the troops. Even the very youngest were helping with the preparation of foods for the ever growing army. Within days Justin's army was growing more skillful than had been hoped, driven by their will to succeed and their love of their country. After a few days Justin and Lynette met with a scribe in the war room to discuss which soldiers were to be chosen to lead the army troops.

"Do you have a total of our troops, so that we know how many units we can accommodate?"

"We will soon have 300 soldiers and 55 horses, my Lord. I have thought a long time about this and I think that we should have a troop of fifty cavalry, with the remaining horses for troop commanders. The infantry and archery troops should also be the same size, which will give us four troops of infantry and one of archers. Do you think that will serve our purposes?" Lynette threw back her long hair as she finished speaking.

"It will have to, we have no other soldiers. Who in the army do you feel is capable to lead each group?" Justin wished that he knew the soldiers better himself. Instead he would have to trust Lynette's judgment.

"For the Archers there is no question. There is a soldier who is the daughter of the chief forester, and she is the best I have seen with the bow. When she was younger she won the king's tournament against the best archers of the time. Although she only joined the army since the rodent attacks started, the archers look to her for guidance in battle. She would be my choice for commander. Her name is Alaynia.

"As for the Cavalry, Blaindoro is the best rider we have. He learned to ride as a youngster since his father was a wealthy merchant in cloth and could afford a horse for him. He joined the army to upset his father, but has stayed because he has gained respect and is a good fighter." Lynette stopped for a moment as she remembered Blaindoro's first days in the army. He had come expecting everything to be brought on a platter, but quickly learned that he would only succeed by his abilities. Since that turn of events he had gained many admirers for his skill at battle and horsemanship.

"For the other three infantry units I recommend Brandalon, Jason and Katarina. Brandalon comes from a poor woodcutting family, and joined the army to help them when his father died. He is blunt and to the point, but for this the other soldiers respect him. Between him and Blaindoro there is a strong team bond. They fight well together.

"Jason was raised in the army. His father was one of your father's commanders who was killed in one of the early battles with Deirdre's mice. He was brought up to know the tactics and skills of a soldier and commander. Of everyone he knows the most about war.

"The person I would recommend as the last commander is Katarina. She is an experienced soldier who fought many battles under your fathers leadership. Unfortunately her troop was all killed but for her. She had been injured and was to rest in bed during a battle. She has blamed herself for this because she was not there. I feel that being a commander would help her overcome this and return to a more active duty." Lynette stopped and looked deeply into Justin eyes.

"These all sound like wise decisions. I will defer to your knowledge and wisdom and agree to these appointments. We shall go now to the training field and promote them in the sight of all the assembled army. Is there anything before we do so?"

"Nothing, my Lord. We should go with all haste." Lynette waited for Justin to rise from his chair then followed his lead. He felt uncomfortable with the formality with which Lynette spoke, but tried to ignore his feelings for the sake of the scribe who followed them from the room. They went immediately to promote the five commanders to the cheers of the army. The bothersome feeling was soon forgotten in the revelry.

***

Justin, only a week into his reign , took some time to survey the food stores and the skills of the growing army. He then called a council with his new team of counselors. As Justin entered the small room he smiled at his assembled team. The war table was now crowded with his new armies' commanders, along with his other advisors. His Aunt, Uncle and sisters were there, the latter smiling as he had never seen anyone smile before. Malcolm sat at the foot of the table across from the King, a renewed look of pride and purpose on his face. Matthew, Mortimer and Sally stood back so as to make room for the crowd of people.

Along with Lynette were the five newly advanced soldiers, each now in command of fifty troops. Alaynia had short dark brown hair and wore a tightly wrapped tunic. Katarina, who sat stiffly in her chair, had light brown hair that fell below her shoulders. Jason was a thin youth with longish blond hair and a certain smile in his eyes that confirmed his pride. Blaindoro sat solidly beside Jason, with a firm look of deference on his face. His hair was a light chestnut brown and fell just above his shoulders. Beside him sat Brandalon with his dark brown, almost black, shoulder length hair. All the commanders smiled in their own way as they watched their King enter. Justin stood at the head of the table, not even seating himself, and spoke.

"The training is coming along remarkably well thanks to all of you, we must continue." The leaders of the army nodded their thanks and agreement. "However, I fear we will soon have a shortage of food and supplies for weapons. We shall have to run a mission to restock our stores, but other issues are more pressing. Firstly, I have noticed in my wanderings that the east end of the town is very open and vulnerable, but Katarina has suggested an idea. Sally, how strong is your thread?"

Sally smiled sweetly as only a spider could. "It can hold a struggling fly at my regular size, I suppose it should hold a large rodent at its current thickness."

"Good, could you set up your web throughout the eastern buildings, good and thick. That should protect our eastern flank." Malcolm thumped the table before Justin could continue. All eyes turned to him as he started to make hand gestures towards Rebekah. She slowly translated the message.

"Malcolm says that if we could also lure the mice into this area from the west we could use it as a trap and back them into it leaving no escape route. Malcolm and I are quickly remembering how we had fashioned this hand speaking, it took us no time at all to remember most of what we use to do and to come up with a lot more useful word gestures. I had almost forgotten how useful it had been."

Rebekah and Malcolm smiled. Justin returned their smile then turned to the two mice.

"Can the two of you please take swords and guard Sally in her duty. You will be able to move around less noticeably than humans would outside these walls." Justin turned to Arthur. "How often do the Ice Wyrms attack, Uncle Arthur?"

Arthur did some calculations on his hands. "It was a fortnight hence. They are due to descend any night now."

"On their next descent I will need some soldiers to collect a large piece of Ice Wyrm flesh. I am assigning this to your group Lynette, have your troop be careful not to touch it with their bare hands."

"Aye, Sir." Lynette displayed a sharp, precise salute to her new King. Justin nodded.

"Once Lynette's troop has obtained the Ice Wyrm segment I will then rely on you, Uncle Arthur, as well as Shanawn and Megan to use it to analyze every substance we have in the castle as we had spoken about. Even every combination of substances. We need to find something we can use as a barrier to hold the creatures back, even if we cannot find something to destroy them." Arthur nodded.

"We shall start immediately to amass all the elements in the castle." Megan smiled quietly with her Uncle.

Shanawn added, "We shall let no stone remain unturned."

"Good, then we shall go back to our respective duties. I fear the witch will leave us little time or room to prepare ourselves." With a smile and a wave of his hand, he dismissed the others from the room, then turned and left himself.

***

The attack arrived two nights later at sunset. When the enemy was still waiting on the horizon, their long shadows looming across the distance to the castle, four troops of Justin's army gathered at his command. As the group awaited the orders of their commander in chief, Arthur and Rebekah drew Justin aside to the stables.

"Since you are at the lead of the army now it will be paramount that the troops can see you to take your commands, my nephew." Aunt Rebekah drew open the door of the stable as she spoke. Standing in the darkened stall was the largest steed Justin had ever seen. It stood nearly twenty hands high at the shoulder, its black head and mane starting from there. As he stared the giant animal tossed back its head, the mane flowing like silk threads. Justin could only marvel as his Aunt continued. "His name is Baldwin, he was your fathers favourite and most reliable until..." She stopped, briefly. "We thought it would be wise and prudent for you to have him at this time." Justin took the reigns of the already saddled and bridled horse and led him from the stall. In one fluid, almost practiced, motion Justin vaulted onto the steed's back before he could even tell what he was doing. Suddenly he was sitting on the horse's saddle, looking over his Aunt and Uncle.

"Thank you, I will take care of him as if he were my own flesh." Justin urged the horse easily from the stable into the courtyard. The amassed men and women looked on without disapproval, they knew from whom they would take orders and did not begrudge him this seat of honour. Shortly, without any time to relish his new position, the battle was upon them.

Two ice Wyrms descended the mountains and closed in on the castle from the north, turning the moat to a sheet of solid ice as they made their way around to the southern front of the walls. The small contingent of Rats and Mice rushed across the hardened water in a frenzy to start beating on the door with a ram.

"Do not wait for them to succeed, drop the drawbridge.", Justin ordered. The descending mass of wood and metal dropped to the ground, capturing several opponents under its mighty weight. Justin held his sword high. "To the battle my friends." And saying so he spurred his horse forward, preceded by the troops.

The mice, not expecting the resistance they faced from Justin's new forces, were immediately on the run from the battle hungry troops. Lynette's force backed one of the Ice Wyrms into a corner of the town where it was trapped and unable to run. Using the swords and spears available only seemed to enrage the beast. Justin, seeing their trouble, turned Baldwin from the retreating mice and charged to her side.

"Try guiding it with flaming torches. Remember you do not need to kill it right now, only capture a piece of its flesh." He turned the horse for a retreat to the front lines.

"Aye, Your Highness, we will try that." Lynette barked out the order to her troop. Compliance was instant. In minutes torches were found and lit, leading the Wyrm where the troop willed.

"Lynette," she turned to him again, "you do not need to call me 'Sir' or 'Your Highness', we have been friends a long time."

"Yes, I suppose we have Justin. Its good to have you back." She smiled, then returned to her warriors. They had been unable to speak privately over the last few days. Justin was glad to have broken the tension.

As he turned the rest of the army was riding back to the castle. The remaining mice had fled into the hills and the other Ice Wyrm had followed. Lynette's troop had quickly removed a boulder size piece from the Ice Wyrm and coaxed it into fleeing by presenting it an opening. The small army returned to the castle.

***

Casualties were few for Balmoria. Only two had been killed and a dozen injured. The best count for the mice was twenty-six dead, and thirty injured but escaped. The battle had been successful. The mice had not expected such resistance from the castle forces. Justin and Lynette stood beside the pieces of Ice Wyrm which Lynette's group had carefully hauled into the courtyard.

"Careful not to touch it, or it will take your hand or a finger." Justin warned the crowd of onlookers. "Blaindoro and Brandalon, have your men and women collect any salvageable weapons from the battlefield, we cannot afford to waste any such resource which is set before us. Have the smiths repair and approve them for use before they are distributed to the soldiers."

"Aye, your highness," the two commanders responded in unison, turning immediately to their task.

"Herald, call Arthur, Megan and Shanawn." Justin bellowed over his shoulder as he watched the two depart with their legions.

"We have come already, my nephew." Justin turned to the smiling faces of his sisters and the care worn face of his Uncle. He had not noticed how worried he looked before.

"Let us get these pieces up to your lab, Uncle. Then we can start our experiments." The flesh was carefully put into boxes and carried to the door of the tower by the troop of soldiers who had collected it. "Strange how the flesh does not bleed, it appears to be only a large mass, like gelatin."

"Yes, Nephew, it is strange, I am sure we shall find more of its strange properties in the next few days. My assistants and I will be in the lab if we are needed. Come up any time Justin, you know you are always welcome." Arthur turned toward the tower.

"I plan to come with you now and offer any assistance I can." Justin followed after his Uncle.

"As you wish, my King." Arthur smiled in his old way. Justin recognized the mischief in his eyes.

"Lead on good servant," Justin chuckled. Shanawn and Megan followed the two, carrying boxes of the substances found in the castle. The mice lifted the heavy crates of Ice Wyrm and ascended the stairs after the humans. The night promised to be long.

***

The night kept its promise, then left before they were through working. The early light of morning had come and gone, and the sun had fully started its ascent into the sky when the small group stopped work for a break. They had slept for only a short time each throughout the night, taking a turn as the clock counted the hours. All but Arthur and Justin. The two were unstoppable as a team and had not worked together for some time. The fellowship was refreshing for both.

"The salt alone does melt the flesh somewhat, but the Peter's salt works better." Arthur noted to Justin as he wrote on his now full tablet.

"The Yellow Burning Stone does a fair treatment of the flesh as well." Justin noted, also taking notes on a writing tablet. "Perhaps if we should combine the two together we may find a more effective combatant for the Wyrms."

Thus followed more hours of trial after trial, mixing the two compounds together. Grinding them to the right powdery consistency. Thoroughly making sure that the mixture was evenly distributed throughout. By late morning they had found what they were looking for.

"When we mix the Peter's Salt with the Yellow Brimstone, in the proper amounts of seven to one, the melting effect is increased ten fold, much more than the two separately." Arthur wrote down the exact recipe for future blending. Shanawn spoke and interrupted the conversation.

"Megan just thought that if the two are ground up and mixed with ground charcoal from the fire they would be easier to transport and then we could spread them on the ground to make a barrier for the Ice Wyrms, then they would not be able to cross it." Megan grinned bashfully from her seat at the workbench.

"One part to the mixture would probably be enough to stabilize it." She smiled shyly, then turned back to her calculations on the bench. The addition was noted to the formula on Arthur's tablet.

"Now we only need to gather these in bulk, where did you obtain these samples girls?" Justin queried the sisters, prepared to record the answer on his tablet. Megan began, but Shanawn started speaking before Megan had the chance to continue.

"The Brimstone is used in the dying of wool by the spinners and weavers. They have a quantity stored, which they have mined in the hills nearby. The Peter's Salt is used by the Slaughterer and Butcherer to preserve the meat for the winter. They collect it from the pile of composting food and animal wastes so that there is little worry of running out." She grinned sweetly from ear to ear.

"And the charcoal would come from burning of wood." Justin finished off the formula. "So the only limiting factor for us is the amount of Brimstone we have before we need to mine some more. Let us collect all that is available in the castle and manufacture as much of this powder as we can. After that Matthew and Mortimer will be responsible to lay it out to circle the castle several times. Be careful not to use it all, we may need to replace it if it should rain. Then we still need a way to stop the mice, this will only hold the ice Wyrms at bay." Justin turned to walk down the steps to the courtyard below, then stopped and turned back. "And thank you all for your work, we have accomplished a lot tonight. Now tell someone how to make this powder, and get some sleep. All of you." Justin strode down the stairs to the courtyard below. Entering the courtyard he saw the tall, slender figure of his brother, standing in the center of the space. He looked better already, since they had stopped watering him daily and increased the heat in his environment. He seemed to wish Justin well from his sun gathering house in the court. Justin smiled back, then turned towards his chambers in the castle for a well-deserved rest.

3
Study

The sun had started to set before the blackened powder had been manufactured and was ready for the two mice to spread in circles around the castle. The night was begun before the first circle was made, but the mice had excellent night vision, which proved to be a powerful benefit for the task. The two rodents worked feverishly and before the stroke of midnight the powder lay in three large circles, centered around the castle. Sally, with Jason's guidance on placement, had strengthened her web traps which were dispersed throughout the eastern village rubble, so that Jason could conduct Malcolm's plan during the next attack. All that was left was to prepare for that attack, and wait. Justin stood on the front castle wall overlooking the rubbled town, a sense of longing and unrest overtaking him. He had not expected this homecoming when he had left for his schooling. He had expected Balmoria, beautiful Balmoria in all her splendor, to greet his return.

Standing on the battlements he worried about many things, things no one dared to speak about. Although they might have found a way to stop the Ice Wyrms, they would soon need to replenish their supplies for this material should it work. Not only would they need to find a way to defeat the ever renewable army of the mice, they would soon have to deal with every magic and enchantment that the witch would send at them if her Mice army failed. He stood for a long time, his thoughts drifting between self pity over his situation, and swelling with pride at the accomplishments of the people against great odds. Then he sighed deeply and stared out over the remainder of his homeland at the rising moon.

"Justin," Rebekah suddenly appeared behind him. "I hope I am not disturbing you too much."

"No Aunt, please join me." Justin motioned with a wave of his hand.

"Justin, I know it has been only ten days since your return, but I must give this to you. I fear that I have left it too long as it is." She held aloft a key, which she had removed from the folds of her clerical cloak. "It is your sacred duty, as the reigning King, to keep the journal of the kingdom and record all that has and will happen in the great book. Your brother, fearing he may die, entrusted the location of this key, and the location of the secret Journal Room, to me for keeping until I could turn it over to the one who should have it. I fear that much of what happened will be lost if you do not take the time now to record it in the book. And the Witch seems to have given us a short break in which you can do this."

Justin took the key from the grip of his aged Aunt and looked at it for a long time. Then suddenly, as if the thought had just occurred to him, he spoke. "Show me to the hidden room." Rebekah turned away quickly, to be followed closely behind by Justin.

***

Although Justin had spent much of his youth exploring the endless hidden tunnels and passages of the castle he had never before found the secret hidden Journal Room. Not that he had not searched. Now, after all those years, he was being led straight to it. Rebekah opened the door to the King's study in the northwestern tower, then locked it behind them. After the mighty oaken door was secured she led Justin over to the massive cases of books, which lined the walls of the room. In the midst of the second shelf from the right, five feet from the floor, was a thick volume with a red and black bound spine. Rebekah reached up and lifted the spine from the bottom. The spine, now lifted away, had concealed a large key hole, the size to fit the key in Justin's hand. He raised the key to the lock, inserted it, and turned it with a mighty effort. The tumblers made an audible click as they turned over and the door swung slowly open of its own accord.

"I have recorded the events from your fathers death until your return. I now leave the rest to you. I will lock the door behind my exit to ensure that none disturb you." Rebekah drifted to the study door. After seeing his Aunt out of the study, Justin turned to the open bookcase, and looked past it to the room revealed beyond.

***

The room was thick with decades, even centuries, of collected dust. Yet for all of this the Kingdom's Journal lay on a high elmwood pedestal in the centre of the chamber, uncovered with the dust, which filled the room. On the shelves surrounding the pedestal were an assortment of written volumes in all sizes, including two shelves containing the entire journal of the kingdom, and six shelves containing the personal journals of the many great Kings and Queens of Balmoria. Each bound and engraved with the seal of the Kingdom. Justin turned from the walls to the book laying open upon the pedestal and turned through the recent pages of history recorded there.

'... Justin, apprentice to the court sorcerer and my third child, left today for his training in the school for

sorcerers. His enthusiasm for the art will be sorely missed until his return ... Mixed news for the kingdom today. The Queen, my fair Carolina, has given birth to two strong and healthy girls today, identical in appearance. Their names shall be Megan and Shanawn. Sadly my fair Queen died in the birth of these two. Her warmth as Queen shall surely be remembered through generations ... There is a hatred and despisal of these my two daughters. Being fourths and twins are seen to be just enough cause, but were it not for the death of my lady these should be overlooked ... There is a joy in the people this season. Never before has there been a growing season of such abundance. The crops are gathered and the annual festival of Samhain is upon us. Such a feast is ours ... A strange, seldom seen, foreigner has taken residence in the mountains of the north. Messages of welcome have remained unanswered. Such behaviour dismays me ... Despite the fair weather and admirable growing season, and the early blooms which have always shown us favour, the crops were low this season. Only by our best wits and fortune will we survive the cold weather now upon us ... The northern foreigner, Deirdre by name, has identified herself as a witch, and the author of this seasons misfortune of crops. A meeting was arranged. This bodes poorly for our fair kingdom ... The castle is attacked by humanesque mice and rats ... The town is destroyed and the people moved into the courtyard ... Jeanetta, my fair daughter and heir is slain in battle. Fury is mine ...'

***

The tale unfolded as it had from his Aunt, a new viewpoint but no new information was to be gotten from this manuscript. Justin thought where he may find some new account of the calamity which he now faced. He turned to the walls around him. Justin looked again through the collection in the shelves until his eyes rested upon the tome which was his father's personal journal. He gently lifted it from its ledge on the bookcase, and placed it on the desk in the corner of the room.

' ...Justin has been gone for less than a year and knows nothing of the joy and sorrow which this day brings me. The joy is for my two daughters born this morning. They are beautiful and bear their mother's eyes. They lay now with the nurse as I write this letter. My sorrow, for it consumes me, is for my wife, Carolina. She has succumbed to the pains of childbirth and has just now passed from this earth. I can find no way to solace myself, but only to record my thoughts and feelings here in my journal. Although I love my two daughters, I shall never be able to look into their eyes without thinking of the death of my fair wife, which has purchased their lives. I do not know how I shall live without her...'

Justin stopped here with tears forming in his eyes. As King his father would not let his love for his wife show or interfere in court business, but truly he had loved her. Justin stopped reading at this point and flipped the pages ahead to his father's personal account of his meeting with Deirdre.

'... An audience with the Witch today in my private chambers. Her demands are too large and her price is too high. She wishes the whole north of the country and half the arable land beneath. When I asked her plans to take this tribute, she swore to raise an army from around us, and that no Sorcerers fabricated enchantment could stop her. At this I laughed since we have had a long standing

friendship between every Kingdom surrounding us. I denied her request and she went into a rant which still has me melancholied. The horrors of which she spoke are not to be believed. She has predicted that I shall see mine own daughter cut down in battle. My son Justin shall not return to see his father and King alive. Peter shall not sit upon the throne of Balmoria. I cannot believe that the Kingdoms around us would rise against us so. I have dispatched letters to all, to ensure their amicable fellowship.'

***

The manuscript stopped short here. No follow up to the entry occurred. Justin wondered what troubles had stopped his father from writing in his diary, since there had been many happenings before his death in battle. Justin turned to the Kingdom's Journal once again for other accounts of battles, which may have taken place with witchcraft in the long and glorious history of Balmoria. He leafed further and further back, through volume upon volume, scanning the hidden record of the Kingdom; finding countless forgotten tales of fortune and hardship, glory and grave. Of hidden treasures and knowledge now forgotten.

'... A Dragon has come to rest in the northwestern Mountains, in a cave overlooking the lake. Many of the Port workers are said to have seen it flying over the northern end of the lake. It is said to be enormous, and its brilliant gold and red body covering is said to be divine to behold. Such a friendly omen we could never have dreamed before ... Large trolls have descended from the mountains and attacked the castle gates. The castle guard has routed them easily. Our hope is that they shall not return ... Of all the kingdoms, in all the worlds, Shalak had to walk into ours.

This vagabond and villain had managed to manipulate a train of donkeys and half a years supply of grain from the peasants before our court magician stumbled upon this dastardly scoundrel's cunning plan. If we shall ever see her again, she shall adorn the walls of our dungeon for a year if not more ...The armies of Talgar the Red have been beaten from Balmoria forever. In today's final battle the mighty ruler to the south has been slain by my daughter Michaela. Joy for the victory, and sorrow for the many fallen of Balmoria, have been intermingled into a celebration and vigil for the dead which may last for many days ... Pirates have once again attacked our merchant ship in search of booty. Much to their surprise our archers held their own against the onslaught of the villains. The attacking vessel fled and our own sloop continued to port where our grain and cloth fetched a fair price at market. The return trip was uneventful ... Cardonia to the south has requested troops of soldiers to help defend her western border from the advances of the Glamorgain horde under the command of Rachel the White. Five troops have been dispatched to take up the fight for our neighbours to the south ...'

***

The morning sunrise had come and gone, the noon sun had risen and set, and the moon was coming out again, when Justin found that which he sought. The history of King Jacobis, the twenty-ninth ruler over Balmorain, the Kingdom which existed before Queen Melanie, thirty-sixth ruler, split the Kingdom between her twin Firstborns, Cherylynn and Jonathan. Cherylynn had inherited the Queenship of Baltain to the east, and Jonathan had come to be the First King of Balmoria on the western coast. It was Jonathan who had set up the three child Monarchy involving Rule,

Cleric and Magician, a system also adopted by His Sister to the east. But decades before this, King Jacobis had recorded some of his struggles, and victories, with a witch that threatened the Kingdom. And Jacobis had not only been a King, but a Sorcerer as well. Justin turned and found his Journal easily in the chronology of manuscripts on the wall shelf. He placed it amid the pile of volumes on the desk and, opening it to the first yellowed page, began the narrative printed in his forefather's steady hand.

'Began reign today over Balmorain. The funeral Pyre of my father lays cold in the mountains. He shall be missed. I hope only that I may rule as well as he ... The season has been good again for my kingdom. The pre-winter feast still rings with song and dancing as I write this note ... It was a cold day in Balmorain. An Auslander has been seen dwelling in the mountains to the north. There are those who claim her a witch ... The witch made her presence known today. All crops withered in their place in the field, and two newborn calves died for no explainable reason. An embassy has returned from her lair with no news of her purpose, only a demand to speak personally to myself. I needs go to her cell tomorrow at noon day ... The kingdom is her demand, a demand which I cannot accept. With every strength that is in my body, and every resource at my disposal, shall I stop this witch at any cost ... A blockade of thorns surrounds the kingdom, such that they dull sword and axe when put to them, and grow anew in moments should a branch be harmed. Replenishment of our low food supplies is impossible. Soon we shall die if this foul business is not ended ... A Daughter, the witch has a daughter who is her apprentice. And one so comely that

she is a pleasure to behold. She did come to me in my chambers last eve, how I know not, with regrets for her mother's actions and offers of help. She did leave me with notes and letters containing certain spells and potions, and their remedies. The whole night I did read with her and understand much of the writings. Near morning she left me to return to the cave of her mother. How, from the loins of that inhuman beast, could come this which is pure and good I know not, but I am glad for her help ... The wall of thorns has withered by the powder made from her notes. I say her for I know not the name of our benefactor. Food has been brought from nearby Cardonia in the south. This siege has ended ... Locusts arrived today to devour the grains in the fields and that stored in our granary. A smoke spell from the letters has driven them to the four corners of the earth ... Today boils appeared on the skin of my soldiers, such that it pained them to raise even their arms. A salve of Juniper has cleansed their affliction ... Our saviour's name is Sycamore. Named for the tree, which grows to the south. How lovely that name ...'

***

The moon had left her place in the sky and the next evening's sun was already low on the horizon when Justin finished reading the account of the sieges and battles of King Jacobis' personal Journal. What wonders he had read, and what wonders he had yet to learn. His progenitor's trials had ended in a long and prosperous reign, wed to the witch's young daughter/apprentice once the tiresome business was through. One thing from the story kept nagging on his mind, the loss of the magic which had helped to stop the witch in the dim, dead past. He held little hope for the return of this knowledge from the grave.

Though his eyes were heavy with sleep, and his body weary with hunger and thirst, he turned once again to the shelves surrounding him. His eyes searched frantically for any source of help in his desperate state. The words from his father's Journal, read far earlier in the evening, or was it the previous evening, stood in his memory as if they were just being read fresh- *'...no Sorcerers fabricated enchantment could stop her.'* His eyes fell on a volume, which stood out from the others by its odd placement. The title of the book stood out all the more - **'The Earth Magic of Witchcraft - A Sorcerer's Guide to Understanding.'**

4
The Battle Joined

Justin had secluded himself for three days without food, water or sleep. No one had interrupted him in his study as he read, cover to cover, the book written by his forbearer, Jacobis of Balmorain, and his wife, Sycamore. He closed the thickly bound text and looked through the windows of the library. It was again becoming night as the sun lowered on the horizon, and the moon began her rise. There was a knocking on the study door, then a loud click as the key turned in the lock. Around the corner of the door appeared his Aunt's head. She spoke softly, not meaning to disturb.

"My apologies, Justin, but the mice gather to attack from the east and south. Your troops await their leader." With this she turned from the room. Justin rose, locked the door to the private journal room, turned wearily and followed his Aunt from the Study. Under his arm was the large volume he had taken so much time and care to read over the last several hours. Hurrying through the halls to the armory and stables, Justin ensured that they stopped to see Arthur before the assault.

"Take this volume, Uncle, and please copy it. You as well as Shanawn and Megan. Make three copies, and know the book well. After we have routed the attacks of the mice, we shall all need all to know the magic that is in these books to fight the powers of the witch. She only holds back now in the hopes that we shall fall under the pressure of her rodent onslaught." Without a word Arthur took the book and nodded. Justin turned back to his purpose. Even if he should fall tonight, the future safety of his Kingdom and people was safeguarded.

***

The army was amassed on the castle bailey when Justin arrived. All fully armed and ready to do battle with the enemy. Justin, astride his mount, Baldwin, addressed the troops.

"Fair fighting, my legions, may we meet again at the end of this contest. Sentry, what strength is their army?" Justin lowered himself from his mount to hear the news delivered. Present were the commanders; Matthew, Mortimer and Sally; Arthur and Rebekah; and Malcolm. The later unrolled a map of the castle and surrounding area for the Sentry to mark.

"There is a troop coming from the southwest, near the lake. Another directly from the south. Two from the southeast and one from the east. All have fifty armed soldiers. The troop to the east also has three Ice Wyrms in its numbers." As he spoke the markings were added to the map. "They seem to wait before advancing further. Perhaps they are wary from their previous defeat." Justin turned to Malcolm.

"What is our strategy, old friend? And be quick so that we may use their fright to our advantage." Malcolm quickly alternated between signs and drawing on the map to relay the message he gave. Rebekah translated for him as he laid out the plan of defense.

"We will take a one on one defense for this battle. The southeastern troop will be attacked by Katarina's infantry units. Hold them from the port road if you can, this would give them easy access to the west end of the village. The southern troop will be taken by Lynette's infantry.

Lynette will be the area commander for these two sections of combat. The hills in this area would detract from the use of the Cavalry, so infantry will be the key to this assault."

"The two troops in the southeast will be met by the cavalry of Blaindoro and the infantry of Brandalon. This will be a flat terrain attack, perfect for Cavalry. The Cavalry will spearhead this assault since they will be our greatest asset in this attack."

"The infantry units of Jason, with the help of Sally, Matthew and Mortimer, will carry out the ambush of the troop to the east. Jason's infantry will split in two. Half of the troop will meet the offensive and will fall back into the eastern arm of the city, followed by the mice infantry. When they are in the streets the remaining infantry will join them in the western end of that section of the city. Matthew and Mortimer will attack from the rear unnoticed and Sally will block off the eastern escape route with her webs, leaving the only escape through Jason's infantry unit. The Ice Wyrms should be stopped from entering the town by the blackened powder circle which the sorcerer's invented and Matthew and Mortimer have lain just outside the town perimeter. Jason, use the buildings to your advantage, and the rodents curse."

"Alaynia's archers will take the eastern and southwestern walls of the castle. They will take any mouse warrior that comes within bowshot of the castle. Archers are essential to the outcome of Jason's fight as they shall have clear shots from the southeast tower. Fires are being lit on the northeast, southeast and southwest towers as we speak to bring light to our mission. On your signal there are three brush piles to the east, west and centre of the town, which can be lighted by a flaming arrow to illuminate our efforts more. Any questions my King?" Malcolm lifted his head towards Justin.

"None Malcolm. This is a fine plan." Justin rested his hand on the old soldier's shoulder. "I hope to congratulate you on a fine defense when we are through." With that Justin leapt to the back of his steed. The tiredness he felt from his lack of sleep was replaced by a rush of vigor and excitement for the battle ahead. He turned his horse toward the castle gates. "Open the Portcullis and drop the drawbridge!"

***

Justin's army struck like a lightning bolt. The Cavalry offensive on the two mouse troops to the east thundered across the plain between the two armies, followed closely by the infantry. The trained horsemen plunged through the sea of hair, teeth, and nails, their spears piercing the breastplate or skull of many a victim. Those that survived the first assault by those on horseback were met quickly by Brandalon and his infantry soldiers, cutting through the legions with sword and axe. Then the cavalry turned and the small remaining troop of mice were surrounded on two sides. Uncertain as to their defense in this situation they tried desperately to fight their way to freedom, cutting with sword and stabbing with spear.

"Blaindoro, you take your troop to the south and I will cover the northern escape." Brandalon hollered over the din of the battle.

"OK, Brandalon, good luck." Blaindoro waved a salute, then his face turned from delight to horror. "Brandalon, get down." His hand reached to him across the field.

The spear hit Brandalon like a juggernaut, knocking him from his horse. The pain only fleeting as he lapsed into unconsciousness. Blaindoro ran to his friend, the troops were distracted for a brief moment, and the ten remaining mice took this chance to break through the hole in the defense and into the northern hills. Blaindoro looked from the body of his fallen comrade, to the escaping mice, then at the battle being staged by Lynette.

"Let the remaining mice go, they cannot harm us if they are running scared. You five men take Brandalon into the castle. The rest of you follow me. Lynette's battle needs help." Blaindoro spurred his mount across the fields to the battle in the south.

***

Lynette's troops were in trouble. The Mouse troops had been joined by a third mass from the northwest, badly outnumbering the defending forces. The castle soldiers had been pushed back nearly to the limits of the town walls.

"Katarina. Take your troops and pull back, you can defend from there if we are overrun. We will need your help if we are forced among the building walls." Lynette, battle weary and bruised, pulled her troops back to the town walls. Arrows flew from the bows of the archers and over the heads of the troops, slightly diminishing the mouse's numbers and keeping them at some distance, but this alone would not defeat them. Lynette prepared her troops for one last charge.

***

From his place atop Baldwin Justin could see the troubled troops of Lynette and her group but was unable to bring assistance. As he watched in helpless desperation the call came from the east. Brandalon had fallen, but the mice had been routed. The remaining soldiers hurried to Lynette's aid. Justin turned his attention momentarily to the Battle in the east Town.

***

The trap amidst the walls of the town had flowed perfectly. The troop of rats and mice, outnumbering half of Jason's troop two to one, had egotistically pushed the infantry soldiers into the town walls, leaving their Ice Wyrm escorts in screaming pain at the edge of the town, unable to move across the line of powder for the burning pain it inflicted.

"We can thank the God that the twins were able to find that barrier from the Ice Wyrms." One of the infantry soldiers stated to Jason. "If not, we could never have hoped to win this battle."

"I had my doubts about twin fourths at first, but after this I have no reservations about having more than our share of Sorcerer's. The two mice and the spider are becoming more useful than I had ever thought as well. After laying the traps with them, I have changed my mind about the initial distrust I had of them." Having said this Jason returned to the task at hand. He instructed his soldiers to allow the rodents to force them amongst the town walls.

Once the mouse warriors were fully within the walls, in the wink of an eye, Sally had completely sealed off the east end of the street just as the remainder of the troop had stepped into the street behind the men and women led by Jason. Turning to see their only escape route blocked the rats and mice panicked, many dropping their weapons, and tried to flee by climbing over walls or through the web. The latter stuck instantly. In a matter of minutes it was over. The volley of arrows from the archers was helpful but unnecessary, the troop of fifty mice were slaughtered to a rodent. The battle in the town was over before it began.

***

Meanwhile, the southwest battle pressed on. The addition of the troops lead by Blaindoro were scarcely enough to push the Mouse Warriors back ten lengths from the town. Many of the troops, trained but unseasoned soldiers, were soon weary from the strain of battle. Once again the troops were pushed back to within the western walls of the town. Here the darkness of the night would do them no favours against the night vision of the Mice. Justin called to the archers on the castle wall.

"Light the brush pile on the west end of the town to bring light to the battle, this may help to blind the Mice also," called Alaynia from the castle wall. Within seconds an arrow was wrapped in cloth, soaked in oil, and sent flaming through the air towards the brush pile, lighting the tinder instantly.

As the tinder lit, much to the surprise of everyone, so did the blackened powder. It flared up with a loud crack as the flames from this ring shot into the air. Circling the castle where the powder had been laid nights before was a short wall of flame. To the east the Ice Wyrms, still trying to cross the painful barrier, screamed as the powder which had melted into their flesh burst into flames. Rolling and crawling the creatures turned from their one minded assault on the castle and headed back to their caves. To the west, several mice which had been standing near the now blazing ring, had caught fire and ran around frantically trying to extinguish the flame. This action only fanned the flames higher as they flickered through the hair on their bodies. One burning creature stumbled closer to the castle as

Justin's troops stood in astonishment, unable to move. As he neared the castle Lynette turned from watching the flaming rodent, the called to the soldiers watching in awe.

"Everyone, back from the second ring. Quickly." Her call came only seconds before the mouse stepped onto this line and set it blazing also. Three of the castle soldiers caught on fire, soon to be extinguished by the others nearby. The mice screamed and turned from the castle. As they ran the archers took those near enough to be hit. Some ninety mice escaped into the hills nearby.

"Quickly, everyone. Gather any weapons which are easily found and meet in the courtyard of the castle. Gather and count the wounded and dead, we shall meet within the hour. Move." With this said Justin turned to the drawbridge as it lowered into place. The eerie cries of the Ice Wyrms and retreating Mice could still be heard. Again the Soldiers of Deirdre had been handed an unexpected defeat, and they would not be able to retrieve their weapons from the field of battle. Justin worried about the retaliation that lay ahead.

***

Each commander reported the fitness of his troop to Malcolm as they entered the room and took their seats. When everyone had gathered Justin addressed them, once again weary since the exhilaration of battle had gone.

"Well done, my commanders. A battle well fought and won." Justin sat at the head of the war room table, smiling a tired smile, and surveyed the weary people around him. "And as I had expected, Malcolm, my congratulations on a splendid plan." Malcolm nodded his thanks. "How fares Brandalon?"

"He is resting in his bed. The spear pierced his shoulder and broke his bones, but they should heal well. There is someone watching him now to see if the blow to his head from the fall has done him any harm." Rebekah looked somewhat concerned for the soldier as she spoke. "All wounded and dead from our company were removed from the field and blessed by myself. The bodies of the mice still litter the field."

"We shall gather and burn them at first light. Malcolm, what are the total casualties for the army?" Malcolm consulted his calculations. Then, turning and speaking through Rebekah, he reported his results.

"Of two hundred infantry in four troops, one hundred and fifty three ready, twenty wounded and twenty-seven dead. One commander lost for battle. Now only three troops of infantry. Of fifty cavalry, twenty-seven riders and thirty-six mounts at battle ready. Ten riders and eight mounts wounded. Thirteen riders and six mounts dead. All Archers ready. We were fortunate that the mice had no projectile weapons to attack with."

"Excellent. Katarina, since your infantry sustained the most damage, you shall take the lead of Brandalon's troops. Your remaining soldiers will join with Lynette's under her lead. All are to stand down for some much needed rest. I feel that the mouse army will not trouble us for some time. Matthew and Mortimer please replace the powder circles around the castle. Archers are to stand guard on the castle walls for the next days. That is all."

With this Justin turned and departed the room. Arthur, Megan and Shanawn met him half way down the hall.

"Come my nephew, we have a surprise that I think will please you." Justin followed his Uncle and sisters to the magician's tower. Just inside the walls they held his sorcerer's staff towards him. As he took and examined it he found a small knot that had not been present before.

"What is this?" he exclaimed as he stroked the wooded knot.

"Push it and find out, but please turn the end away from us." Arthur directed the top of the staff away from the small assembly. Justin pushed the button. Instantly fire burst from the top of the staff for the distance of five armlengths, and a blue smoke filled the corridor. Justin stood in awe, unable to speak.

"We have fitted a small charge of blackened powder in the shaft and installed a striker for lighting it. When you meet the forces, as you suspect, you will have some tricks that they could not foretell in store for them." Arthur smiled his winning smile. Justin could not help returning it.

"Thank you all. This will come in handy when I meet our hidden friend." Justin turned the staff in his hand. Shanawn spoke.

"It is Megan's design. The staff holds twenty charges and then needs to be refilled. It could be used even to light a fire if necessary." She smiled.

"And the charges are powder wrapped in small balls of paper. They are easily produced, stored and installed without too much attention." Megan pointed to a small opening in the side of the staff as she spoke. "Here is where the balls are inserted. And here are a few replacements to use for now. They produce smoke of differing colours." She handed him a small bag of round pellets.

"Thank you again. We need to make more of this powder, now that it has more properties than just stopping Ice Wyrms. In a few days some of the troops will accompany us into the mountains to mine more Brimstone. If you could find out where it is mined before then, we shall have an easier time of finding it." With that Justin turned down the hallway. "I shall see you in the morrow my friends, please study the spells I have given you. They shall be the salvation of us soon I am sure." With this Justin turned the corner and stumbled off to his chambers for a well deserved, and easily realized, night of sleep.

5
Magic Duel

Justin slept, undisturbed, into the following noon. When he awoke from his slumbers the pyre for the mice soldiers was already dying outside the castle walls, the powder circles were replenished, and the remaining soldiers were practicing their skills on the castle bailey. The army was weary, yet happy with the victory, and pleased to be preparing themselves to fight again for their new king. Justin wandered aimlessly through the courtyard, staff in hand, casting a winning smile at all he met. He approached a group of archers on the castle wall.

"How goes your training, my companions." Justin walked to the group. They advanced a sharp salute, as their group leader spoke.

"It goes well, your highness. The new recruits are doing better than any had hoped, and I for one have lost my doubts about the animals, which we have now working with us. They fought well in the last battle. How fairs Brandalon?"

"He is recovering well, from last report. I had received word of his condition just after waking today."

"We shall certainly miss his skill. I have heard many speak badly about his temperament, a bad one as I have witnessed myself, but he is a skilled commander and fighter, that is sure. I would follow him to the underworld if need be, and certainly come back alive."

"Thank you, comrades, continue with the excellent work," with a quick salute he continued on his way. As he continued along the top of the ramparts Rebekah approached him at length.

"I hope you slept well, Justin. The army has been busy with activity all morning, after the victory last eve. All have nothing but praise for you. How goes the strategy for our full defense?"

"All is well now, my aunt. I only hope that we are prepared for the treachery that this witch will cast upon us when she sees that her army will not overthrow us." Justin smiled with pleasure over the advances of his people in the past few weeks. "What think you of the events thus far?"

"Our fate could have been much worse. I thank the God that you were here to guide us when no one else could. I feared for our survival when your brother was turned. I now fear only for your brother. How shall he be returned to us?"

"In time we shall find a way. For now the safety of the kingdom, and the people in it, are our primary concern. Peter would have wanted it thus. Come, we must attend the cremation of our fallen." With this he held out his arm. Gripping it, his aunt allowed him to escort her to the castle entrance to join with the others gathered there for the rites of those deceased in battle.

After the pyre was ablaze and the fallen warriors were fully engulfed in flames, Justin turned from the fire to let the grieving families and friends to their own. He returned to the castle, and ascended the stairs to the study. Before the events left his memory, and while the Witch still left him some free time, he wanted to sit and record the events from his return. This took him most of the daylight hours, but just prior to the evening meal he finished his tale. Justin replaced the books and writing utensils to their places, locked the door to the secret room, and entered the hall. Locking the great study door behind him. He turned to see Lynette standing in the corridor in front of him, smiling.

"I have been searching everywhere for you, Justin. Come, please, and share a meal with me while we talk of your time away." She approached and gave him a friendly kiss on the cheek. "I hope I am not being too bold or presumptuous?"

"Not at all, my fair Lynette. I would be honoured to share a meal with my country's most loyal and beautiful guardian." They turned down the passageway towards the castle dining hall, laughing as they went.

***

The meal passed pleasantly, the old friendship rekindled by the humour of the two and the ease of the conversation. Lynette told of her days after Justin had left, when she was new in the army, and how it had been a slow and difficult climb to the rank of commander with so many excellent candidates present. She told about how Blaindoro came to join the castle forces in defiance of his father, after his brother took over the family cloth business, and how she had been the one to notice his skills and help develop them. Justin in returned told tales of the school of sorcerers and the many scholars he had met there. After the two had eaten and drank their fill, they found themselves walking along the walk atop the curtain wall surrounding the castle and her inhabitants.

"Justin, what are our plans for the future. How shall we fair in the next attack?" Lynette, her silken hair shinning golden in the light of the setting sun, looked worried as she leaned against the outer masonry of the wall.

"Tomorrow, if you have warriors that can be spared, I would like you to send an armed force into the hills to mine some more of the brimstone used to make the blackened powder. I think that this will help us in our future fight with the Witch. However, I fear that she will now attack us with more that just an army of mice. I fear that we will now have to deal with the full power of her magic spells and incantations."

As if in answer to Justin's words, storm clouds started to form on the horizon. Ominous looking clouds, which predicted a storm like no other that could be remembered in the tiny kingdom. Justin gazed for a moment at the gathering of the clouds, the colours were blacker than any he had ever seen before in his lifetime. The flash of a lightning bolt and the crack of thunder following it closely declared that the storm was almost upon the castle. Justin knew in his heart that this storm was to be like no other that the small kingdom had ever seen.

"We should gather in the confines of the castle walls. If I do not miss my guess she even now raises a mighty storm to wield against us." With this Justin led the astonished commander towards the stairs. "Herald, call all the people to find shelter. A terrible storm mounts against the castle. All able hands are to be at the ready for whatever lies ahead."

The storm lashed against the walls of the castle, soaking the ground in the courtyards to a thick mud instantly, and forming small rivers in the ground of the castle bailey. Justin rushed to the tower stairs leading to the rooms of his Uncle. He threw open the door and raced up the stairs. Arthur sat in the centre of the room leafing through a large book. Hearing Justin approach he raised his head.

"Justin, how good to see you. This book is fascinating to read, I am so glad that you found it. Herein is strange magic, yet it is amazing. However, I fear that the recipes are long to read and understand, and shall not be quickly or easily copied. We have unbound the book so that we can all read it in stages. How are you faring with your copies , girls?" Arthur turned to the twins sitting at benches in the corner of the room. Justin only now realized their presence.

"I have barely finished reading the original now, but Megan has concluded her reading and completed a listing of the spells in the book. She is now amassing the more popular essences in the spells from those we collected for the blackened powder." She smiled her broad grin.

"I can see that most are present here. Some of the more obscure ones we will have to collect further, if we can find them." Megan sat at a table completely covered in bottles, jars and containers.

"The Witch has already started her mischief upon us. Is there a spell contained in the book for calling and calming a storm?" Megan pulled forth a piece of paper, which she had laid on her desk.

"This is Megan's listing of the spells in the book, including which page they are on. It should make our searching much easier than otherwise." Arthur awaited the word of his apprentice.

"The spell for calling a storm is on page 15. It lists no counter spell." Justin's heart sank as he heard the young girls words.

Justin then heard the most scattered noise than any in his memory. He looked through the window to find a rain not of water, but stone. The Witch had called this storm and turned the water to small stones with which to beat the castle walls and injure those caught in the shower.

"There is a spell for turning water to rock. The reversing spell is to take three powders which we already have and to burn them with Hickory wood." Megan was already taking the containers of powder from the bench as she stopped speaking.

"You mix the powders, I shall have some troops gather Hickory wood in the castle courtyard. I shall meet you there to light the fire." Justin raced down the stairs and left his Sisters and Uncle to combine the powders for the spell.

The soldiers, pelted with rocks as they worked, quickly assembled the required wood and piled it high in the courtyard. Megan joined Justin carrying a small sack in her hand. Two of the soldiers took the sack at Justin's command and threw it onto the fire. Dust filled the air for a few moments as the two turned from the woodpile and ran for the cover of the battlements. Justin stepped forward, staff in hand, and addressed the heavens.

"Blow winds from the east and west. Turn this rock to water again." With these words spoken fire shot from the end of his staff, setting the wood ablaze. Smoke filled the courtyard in billows, every where it touched that was magically turned rock, returned to water. Including that which was still falling from the sky. The water threatened the fire itself, but the powders in it kept the fire burning and the smoke billowing. The crowd looked on in amazement, then let up a cheer. Justin turned from the fire after a long time, then walked back into the castle to his Uncle and sisters.

"The chant was a good touch, Nephew. Even I almost believed that you had conjured up the fire." He smiled at Justin.

"Five parts out of a hundred are what you do. Ninety-five are what others thought you did." Justin smiled and laughed at his own ability to play the game. A game he had not played since his return. In a few hours, presumably when the Witch discovered that her spell had been foiled, the storm died away and the last of the water, which had been pouring into the castle, drained away. Balmoria had won the first magical battle in this fight.

***

After a fitful night of rest a small troop ascended the mountains, lead by the Spinners and Weavers, to collect some more of the precious brimstone that the castle needed. The guard stood watch over the work crew as they dug the foul smelling substance from the ground and piled it into satchels and carts for transport back to the castle. Justin met them at the drawbridge upon their return.

"How faired your expedition?" Justin queried the commanders as they approached. Katarina spoke.

"We have retrieved more of the yellow brimstone as required. I am not sure if it was just our nerves, but it felt like someone, or something, was watching us as we worked. I would not like to repeat the trip, your highness." She gave him a staunch salute and continued to lead her troop into the castle. The worry in her eyes could not be disguised.

The brimstone was given to the blackened powder makers who immediately started on a new batch of the miracle concoction for future use. On Justin's order the drawbridge was again raised into place.

***

After a wait of five days, nothing more happened in the way of magic. The people of the castle were becoming nervous, and anxious about what may lie ahead. Justin woke early one morning and toured the castle wall walks asking the guard what, if anything, had happened through the previous night.

"Nothing Sire. The night was quiet, and the morning fog unusually thick. Now that the sun begins to rise you can see that there are green patches in the fields around the castle. The Witch seems to have given us favour rather than horror from her last spell. All that rain has caused the crops and grass to grow again. You do not suppose that she has withdrawn in the face of your superior magic? "

Sure enough Justin looked out over the fields and valleys that surrounded the castle to the east, south and west, only to see that the green of the grass was once again visible where there had been only bare rock and ground only days before. Something that disturbed Justin twinged in the back of his mind.

"Does the morning fog not wait until the sun rises before it is melted away?"

"Yes Sire, it does normally. And as I said it was unusually thick this morning. You do not suppose it means anything, do you?" Justin smiled at the young soldier.

"I do not know, but one thing is for sure. The witch did not do us any favours by her own choosing." Justin begged his leave of the man and continued his walk along the castle wall.

By noon time the grasses had reached a height of four fingers. Justin, and everyone else in the court, knew that this was no ordinary grass. Blaindoro was sent to gather a sample for the magicians to work with. He returned to the castle minutes later with bleeding cuts covering his hands and legs.

"The blades are as stiff and as sharp as, well, as blades. They would make an excellent short sword, and judging by their height now, an excellent long sword by evening. I tried your highness but I could not snap one from its roots." Blaindoro followed Rebekah to the castle infirmary to bandage his wounds.

"Uncle, this sounds like the razor grass from the book. I believe there is a liquid we can make which can be sprayed onto the leaves to wither the plants. Shall I prepare some?" Megan had finished copying, and had evidently been studying and memorizing, the spell book over the past few days.

"Yes my child. Prepare at least several barrels full. I am sure we shall need that much for this quantity of weeds, if not more. Shanawn, you shall devise some way to spray this elixir upon the plants themselves. Make yourselves busy, we want to stop these plants as soon as possible so as to keep them from spreading." Arthur looked tired.

"Why do you look so tired, my Uncle? Have the nights been long for you as well?" Justin rested his hand on the arm of his mentor and instructor.

"Yes, my nephew, they have. I have been trying to decipher any patterns in the spells, which may help us to fight against any new spells which have been derived by witches the world over since the book was written. I have found a few in my readings. Perhaps you would care to look over them with me once this crisis is averted.?"

"I would be proud to, Arthur. Nothing would bring me more joy." With this the two sorcerers parted until the apprentices had brewed the spell to rid the kingdom of this new threat.

***

That evening the army used Shanawn's modified blacksmith's bellows to spray the concoction, supplied by Megan, over the offending weeds, which were now at waist height. The troops spent the better part of the night spraying a patch with the liquid, waiting until the stalks drooped and withered, then knocking them down with long poles. They spread out in an ever widening circle around the castle until, early in the morning, they came to the edges of the fields which contained the offending grasses. By this time, these were taller than the tallest soldier who was working in the field because of the time taken for the long and arduous task. Half way through the night Megan mixed a second batch of the elixir for the troops, as the first batch had started to become depleted in the fields. During this time Arthur and Justin, joined by Shanawn and Megan when they were not needed to support the troops in the meadows, poured through Arthur's calculations and cross references of the spells contained in the book.

"I follow your logic unerringly, Uncle. For plant spells diluted urine seems to be the main ingredient for the antidote, along with some form of stimulant for the properties of the liquid such as powdered brimstone or pumice."

"Yes, and for rock spells powdered animal skin seems to have the desired effect." Arthur ran his finger down the column of spell type and remedies. "I hope that this will see us through the tragedies ahead."

"I am sure that this list will come in very handy in the next few weeks." Justin rose from his chair. "Now, it is time for some rest before the morning is upon us. Let us retire now, before another spell should fall on our kingdom." Arthur nodded his agreement. The four staggered wearily down the stairs and retired to their separate bed chambers.

***

Several days passed with no sign of Deirdre's works. All the towns' people waited anxiously to see what the next trial for the team of magicians would be. They could never have dreamed what this challenge would be when it came.

Justin woke the forth morning after the night of the plants. He walked happily down the hall, only to be met with the startled faces of Rebekah and Malcolm rushing down the hall to meet him. Rebekah spoke.

"Ixche grathe themonde." At this she stopped short, lowering her head as she gave a great sigh. Justin's look of confusion had stopped her in mid sentence.

"What is it you are saying, Aunt Rebekah?" Justin could tell that the two could not understand his speech by the looks in their eyes. Rebekah turned towards Malcolm.

Malcolm started to speak in his exaggerated gestures. Although not as proficient at reading the mans hand signs as his Aunt, Justin slowly understood the message he was relaying. Throughout the castle every man, woman and child could not speak to each other for the differing language each tongue uttered. Justin took to a run down the hall and started to pound on the doors of his Uncle, and Sisters. The three came into the hall, Justin addressed them.

"We must consult the book. The peoples of the castle can no longer speak to each other and I fear that the Witch will use this as an opportunity to attack." Justin could tell his words were of no use. The three magicians stood in awe, staring at the utterances of their friend and relative.

Justin tried to use the same hand gestures mastered by Malcolm. Slowly the three began to understand. Megan clapped her hands and spoke.

"Morthre." She stopped, suddenly remembering that no one could comprehend her speech. She stooped to the ground and started drawing in the sand. The others gave a cheer, which could be understood in any language. The words she wrote were; 'Babel - Page 32'

***

As Justin had feared the sentry soon brought a note that Deirdre's army, one hundred and fifty strong, had begun to gather on the horizon. Justin relayed his orders to his commanders as quickly as he could write. The army was to be amassed and readied. Arthur, Shanawn and Megan were collecting the ingredients for the spell to loose their tongues once again. The troops, trained and able to understand these simple orders no matter how they were given, armed themselves and gathered on the castle bailey for action.

As the soldiers had finished preparing themselves, the three came into the courtyard with a sack of leaves and sticks and a long train of people carrying arm loads of branches which they piled in the center of the courtyard. The sack was emptied onto the pile and Justin lit the heap with his staff, uttering some words unintelligible to the amassed people. The thick smoke filled the air, Arthur, Megan and Shanawn breathed deeply of the heavy odour. As they spoke, all could understand their language.

"Everyone, breath deeply the smoke from the fire. Warriors first, as they will soon need to defend us against the gathered hoard." Arthur's words commanded instant compliance. Soon the Archers were on the walls and the foot and mounted units were ready to flow from the castle door when the mice closed in. They waited just long enough.

The mice, prepared for a defenseless force that could not organize itself, foolishly swarmed across the moat to the castle walls and tried to erect siege towers to climb the walls. Before they knew what was happening fifty arrows flew through their ranks and felled several dozen soldiers.

In the confusion that followed, the castle drawbridge dropped among a group of the armed rodents and the infantry units streamed out of the castle amidst the astonished and unprepared mouse troops. They soon realized that the army they fought could easily relay messages and fight with great strength against them. Many fell in the bedlam as the mouse commanders realized that they had been mislead by Deirdre.

As the castle army pushed the rodents back against the northern walls of the western town Arthur approached Alaynia on the castle wall walk.

"I have a surprise for the king. If you would be so kind as to have your best archer send a flaming arrow into that wooden cask by the town walls." Alaynia called over Aaron, her most accurate archer, and relayed the message. "I think we shall all see a wonder should he hit it."

The arrow flew through the air, effortlessly hitting its mark. The resulting explosion tore through the ranks of the mice and caused the army of Justin to drop back to their knees. A dozen mice were felled in the blast as shards of metal ripped through the air. Justin's soldiers fell back at his command.

"There is one about three lengths down the wall to the west. If you think you can hit it." At Arthur's command another arrow was set ablaze and sent thought the air to the barrel beneath. At the sound of the explosion, the remaining mice that could still run turned from the castle and fled. Some two dozen escaped the arrows of the archers and managed a retreat to the hills. The night was soon quiet as the withered and dried razor grass, which had been set ablaze by the explosion, silently spread fire through the fields surrounding the castle.

***

"What was that, Arthur, and do not try to deny that you had any part of the action." Rebekah cross examined her brother as Justin, the commanders and the twins watched. The two mice and Sally were re-laying the circles of blackened powder, which were lost in the resulting blaze. The army had returned to the castle after clearing the field, and was retiring for the night.

"It was just a barrel of the blackened powder which was mixed with some rusty nails and such that were left laying around the castle. I had calculated the distance they would fly and made certain that none of the soldiers of Balmoria were within range. It is a formidable weapon, do you not think?" Arthur sat back into his chair, an unaccustomed look of pleasure and pride across his face. Justin could not hold back a laugh.

"Stand down, Rebekah. It was an effective ruse, you must admit. I only wish he had shared his little secret with all of us before he carried out his plan. I dare say we may be able to use his new found device again before we are through with this fight." Justin patted his Aunt on her shoulder.

"I suppose you are right, Justin. But it gave me a fright as I watched the flames rise into the sky. I suppose it also served its purpose to frighten the mice. And as a bonus it has rid us of the dried weeds left on the fields. It was a good contraption you made." She offered her hand for the sorcerer to grasp. He took it warmly.

"Come, everyone, it is late and we may yet share a meal together before we rest." Justin rose from the war room table and preceded the assembly to the dining hall for a well-deserved repast before they retired.

***

The magical attacks by the Witch grew stronger and more frequent, as if she needed less time to prepare her next spell after the previous had failed. The castle water turned salty, the vision of the army blurred prior to an attack, the castle moat turned to blood; all to be remedied by a potion, salve, or a powder. After several weeks of retaliating to the Witch's spells and incantations, Justin met with his Uncle in the King's Study. The aging Magician sat across from the young, reigning monarch.

"Art, I do not know what we are to do. The Witch's powers are strong, and they do not appear to lessen in this fight. Her magic does not follow the rule of five to ninety-five as with sorcerer's magic, her enchantments are as real as they are deadly. I fear that we will soon be depleted for resources, either in the spell book, or in the materials required to cast the counter spells." Justin looked forlornly at his Uncle.

"Perhaps the journals of Jacobis contain some clue as to how he defeated the Witch when he was faced with her."

"I did not see anything on my first examination, and I have not come across anything in my reviews since, however you can look for yourself if you like. A second set of eyes may reveal what the first set overlooked." With this Justin stood up from his chair and walked across to the shelf of books on the wall. He lifted the spine of the red and black bound volume on the shelf, revealing the keyhole. With a turn of the key, the door swung open for the two to enter.

In moments the two were leafing through the personal journal of King Jacobis of Balmorain. They turned through the many pages of the text until they came to the end of the tale of the Witch's escapades and the beginning of Jacobis' married life with Sycamore. Nothing was recorded in between.

"Just as I feared my Uncle, nothing is recorded on the blank page and a half between the two events. As if he had meant to record it later and never perchanced to do so." Justin readied to close the book.

"Not so quickly, my Nephew. Let me try something with the pages of the journal." Arthur walked to the wall and removed a candle that was affixed to a bracket on the wall. Lighting the candle he held it so that the light of the candle shone through the empty pages of the journal. Justin's jaw dropped in amazement as sparkling silver letters appeared.

"What are these word's, my Uncle? From where did they come?"

"There is an ancient form of letter writing that leaves the text invisible to the eyes, until the person does what I have done here. Read what Jacobis has recorded." Justin stood so as the read the now visible text, and read aloud the words on the page.

"I, Jacobis, have chosen to record the following instructions in the hidden letters of the Sorcerer's so as to keep them from those who may destroy my fair Sycamore, yet to keep it for those who may need them in the future.

" As stated in my Journal the Witch was destroyed, and her daughter joined to me in wedlock. This is only true to the masses. Sycamore was the Witch. Sycamore as the Witch was both evil and good, her image changing to suit her temper at any given time. The wicked in her did not know of the existence of the moral, yet the just knew of the sinful. In her attempts to save Balmorain from herself, she had entrusted to me the location of that which witches the world over call the 'Black Stone'. It has the ability to drain the evil powers from a witch should one touch it and the incantation written on its surface be spoken. The thing is hard and black to its core, filled with the most evil magic imaginable. Sycamore bade me retrieve it to remove the evil in her and keep her as her virtuous self.

"The stone may be found, for I returned it from where it came, in a shielded case carved into the rock walls of a cave in a mighty mountain to the west, past the great Sea of Balmorain. There is a natural harbour for to dock a sailing vessel just off the northwestern coast of the Sea. You shall know it by..." At this Justin stopped reading and turned to his Uncle. The salvation of Balmorain was hidden to the west, and once again Jacobis had told them how their salvation was to be found.

6
The Quest Begun

In less than five hours the scuttled sloop in the Harbour of Balmoria was being raised from the harbour floor. The ship had been filled with water early on in the fighting so that the armies of the Mice could not take her from the kingdom. This proved to be a sound decision since the boat was not only undamaged, but the sea water had swelled the planking to make it extremely watertight. The mariners of the Kingdom wasted no time before they set to work on repairing the rigging and sails. Others started to pump the hull to remove the water within, bringing the ship to the surface once again. Still others listed and prepared the provisions for the journey, which lay ahead of them. As the seamen floated the great sailing ship and rigged her to sail, watched over by three infantry units should the mice attack their efforts, Justin once again gathered his military advisors in the great war room.

"Our future success lies in a hidden cave to the west. There will be found hidden a stone which will drain Deirdre's powers and free us from her domination. I must lead this search myself, leaving Rebekah in charge of the castle army, and Arthur and Shanawn in charge of the magical struggle with our worthy opponent.

"For the journey by sea we have but one sailing vessel, and she can hold only sixty-five persons. There are twenty sailors, Myself, Matthew, Mortimer, Sally, Megan, as well as Lynette and twenty-five of her infantry. The remainder shall comprise fifteen archers under the command of Aaron. That will be our full compliment for the journey.

"All others in the army will be lead by Rebekah and Malcolm into any battles that require your proficiency. Some of the sailors have come from your ranks and these positions must be filled with new recruits. This task I leave to you to fulfill.

" I hope that our return shall find us with the stone as well as provisions for the town's people, we shall leave at the first opportunity. The seamen have promised me no more than a three days wait for our vessel to be prepared. Are there any questions?" He surveyed the people gathered in the room, The worry on their faces was easily read. Malcolm dropped his hand to the table with a loud bang, the signal that he was about to speak.

"I think that it is unwise at this point to have two heirs to the throne leave the safety of Balmoria's castle walls. Would it not be better to have Lynette's infantry take on the quest alone?" Rebekah stopped her translation.

"Yes, Malcolm, it would probably be wiser to send either me, or Megan, or neither. However, I must follow on the path of my forbearer where only Kings may tread. As well we may need the wisdom of two sorcerer's on the trip since it will likely be full of mysteries and trials until we acquire that for which we seek. Therefore, I think it is wise to have the two of us on the quest. I have take the most well trained infantry unit to guard our progress, as well as two strong rats and Sally who shall be very useful on our expedition I am sure. I fear there is no other way to handle this situation. I know the risks, but the rewards far outweigh the dangers. I fear I must proceed, against your commendable advice." Justin smiled at his military advisor and long time friend. Malcolm, though reluctant, nodded his agreement across the table.

"If there are no other questions I would ask you all to attend to your duties until we are underway." Justin rose from his chair as it became obvious that no one was about to speak. "Thank you, that will be all."

***

Better than promised the ship was rigged and stocked late after the noon of the second day. Justin called his captain into the war room. He met the still worried faces of the commanders and the rest of the assembly.

"Ethan, you have done well to be prepared in this time. When shall we depart for the western shore of the Sea of Balmorain?" Justin was well pleased with the efforts of his captain.

"We had some good fortune, my lord. We can sail at last light. I think that it may be wise to start our journey without the watchful eye of our visitor." Justin, and the entire assembly, nodded their approval. Ethan bowed low. "If you will excuse me, my Lord, I have some last minute preparations to attend to."

"As do we all. Lynette, Aaron, prepare your soldiers for the journey. Matthew, Mortimer, Sally and Megan, prepare yourselves for the trip. Ethan, we shall see you at the ship at sun set. Until then, fair luck." The group took this time for farewells, knowing that there would be little time left later. Justin turned and strode from the room. The wait did not leave much time, and he had left some matters unattended.

***

Rebekah met Justin in the journal room at his bidding. He held aloft the keys which she had entrusted to him what seemed like many months ago.

"I am leaving you the task to keep the journal of the kingdom until my return. In this leather case I have secured an empty journal, which I have chosen for my own. It may be short, but it will contain all that it must for future Kings to read for the defense of Balmoria." Justin placed the keys into the palm of Rebekah's outstretched hand.

"I will keep the journal safe, you do so with yourself. I have read the runes to glimpse the future, and have found that your trip may be favourable, but will require hard work and perseverance. Do not stray too far from the clear path unless you must. The way may be treacherous, but you have a worthy commander at your side. I have created and consecrated a talisman for you with the Rune for protection, Eolh. It will help to keep you safe on the journey, and to guard your return unharmed." Justin took the talisman from her outstretched hand.

"I will be careful, and wear it always", with this Justin placed the talisman around his neck and embraced his aunt. Justin released his grip and turned to the door. Rebekah followed to see the company on the start of their journey.

***

The party met on the docks, ready for their departure. Ethan commanded his crew to man their stations, let loose the ropes, and slowly the ship pulled away from the pier. Justin, Megan, Lynette, the two rats and Sally waved from the stern of the ship as it cut a path through the calm waters. Arthur, Rebekah, Shanawn and the commanders returned the farewell salute. They stood a long while until the ship could be seen no longer on the horizon, then they silently turned and wound their way east up the road leading to the castle through the western town.

The sloop sailed on into the night. Ethan's sailors guided the prow through the silent waters. The low night breeze aiding their advance. When they were well underway Ethan approached Justin.

"Now that our voyage has started, would you please inform me of our destination, and how we are to get to that point?" The captain was old and experienced enough to command his crew's respect. As well as that of Justin.

"Certainly. We sail straight west until we come into sight of the far shore of the Sea, a five days journey by the instructions in the book. When we can see the shoreline we turn north towards the mountain peaks. At the base of the mountains, hidden in the rocks, there should be a natural dock with a path leading to the northwest. Here we shall weigh the anchor and put ashore. The crew can then wait until our return from the quest."

"You look uneasy, my Lord. Does this quest trouble you?" Ethan stood firmly at the feet of the sorcerer as he lay comfortably on the deck.

"Yes it does, more so than even the sea swells. I truly fear that the way to the sealed cave will not lay revealed for us, nor shall it be easily found or traversed. I fear for the safety and lives of these who have followed me on this quest, all choosing of their own free will once bidden to come." Justin looked upon the tall stalwart sailor.

"In my time I have sailed and fought along side many a man. All were of my choosing and none were easily lost, but lost some were. In that time I have found one great truth. The battle is long, and the road treacherous, but in the end the struggle is within yourself and there lies all the strength needed to overcome." With this the Captain turned and called out directions to his crew. The sails were trimmed slightly, and the ship sailed on.

***

As morning broke the next day the wind died down. The ship suddenly stopped in place in the waveless waters and all was still. Justin came onto deck, sensing that there was a problem.

"What has happened, Captain?"

"The wind has suddenly died, and our sails no longer send us forth. I believe our Witch is playing with us again, for I have never had such an abrupt calm in the northern Sea of Balmorain in my history as a sailor. This is a seaman's nightmare, my Lord, but we have more tricks than she knows." Ethan called to the crew. "All hands on deck. Man the oars." From concealed lockers the sailors pulled ten long, stout poles, flattened on the end. They fitted these to brackets on the edge of the hull and started to pull on the ends. The ship slowly started to move in the water.

"The Witch will be shocked to see us moving even amid her unnatural calm. She has not beaten us this time. We carry these for the calms farther south, and to dock at tight harbours. They shall do us for now." Ethan smiled a wide mouthed grin as he called the tempo for the men. "Stroke, stroke, stroke..."

Justin watched the horizon as the sturdy men hauled on the ships oars. After a morning of taking turns to draw on the poles, Justin called out to the weary men.

"Put away your oars, for we shall have all the wind we want, and then some more." Ethan rushed to his side. "If I do not miss my guess, yonder lies a storm raised by the Witch. It resembles the storm she called against the castle, at best it will throw the ship around and at worst it may likewise turn to rock." As Justin spoke the sailors stowed the oars and started preparations for a storm.

"The ship could not hold out against rocks beating against her planks and sails. The rigging would be damaged for sure. However, if I recall, it was a fire you started to fend off the stones, and the ship is made of pure wood. Such an action would destroy her should she catch fire." Ethan's voice rose as the wind started to pick up and fill the until now empty sail. "We could try to sail ahead of her if this wind picks up, but she is sure to catch us in the end. And we have no safe harbour to head for. What can we do?"

"What does the ship use for ballast to keep her upright?" Justin turned his limited naval knowledge over in his mind.

"We have some large, flat rocks down in the hold to sturdy her. Certainly you are not suggesting...?"

"Yes, have some of your men bring one up to the deck. We shall have to start our fire on the rock. If we have luck with us we can keep it small and contained to the rock, and we shall also continue to soak the boards beneath with water to keep them from igniting. We will leave the lighting of the fire until the last possible moment, in case Deirdre should have neglected to use the rock spell." As Justin spoke three seamen departed to retrieve a stone at their Captain's gesture. By the time he had finished speaking the stone was in the process of being hauled onto the deck.

"I only hope that this works. Should we catch fire we will be done for, sure enough." Ethan barked orders to his crew in preparation for the storm.

The infantry and archers, along with their commanders, remained below the deck. Matthew, Mortimer and Sally insisted on helping Megan with the preparations for the spell. The rats piled wood on the slate table while Sally held the many jars and containers required by Megan for the powder mixture. The powder was added to the wood and a piece of sailcloth draped over it to help keep it dry from the elements. Matthew and Mortimer filled buckets with water and remained at the ready should the fire be lit and get out of hand. Justin stood with his staff at the ready.

In minutes the waves had risen and started to rock the boat. Small stones could be seen breaking the water's surface as the storm raced towards the boat. The sailors rushed to secure rigging and drop the sails. As the small stones started to drop on the deck the rats removed the piece of sailcloth and Justin lit the fire. The smoke billowed into the air, blinding the crew but turning the stones into harmless water. The infantry made themselves busy manning buckets to remove any water from the hold. The threat of rocks had been bypassed, only to be replaced by the threat of fire. The two faithful rats continued to water the deck under the rock to avoid it drying.

After two hours the rocks had stopped dropping into the Sea around the boat outside the power of the smoke, but the storm raged on. Justin extinguished the fire and helped with the bailing of the hold. Throughout the night the storm roared, tossing the ship like a toy. The crew fought against the wind and waves like unstoppable demons, yet still two of the crew and one of the infantry were lost overboard in the violent raging of the sea. As the sun rose on the eastern horizon, the storm started to ebb away.

"Quickly, raise the sail and catch the wind from the end of storm, it may be the last we shall see." Ethan's words, though wise, were incorrect. The winds lessened but still pushed the ship forward towards her destination. Deirdre could not hold control of the weather indefinitely and had lost it.

***

As the ship sailed on, the party of adventurers learned many things about sailing from the captain and crew. Ethan and his sailors were wise and good teachers, and soon the whole party took turns manning the sails and rigging. At the end of the third day, still without sight of shore, a ship was sighted on the horizon sailing towards the Ship of Balmoria.

"Quickly, stow the infantry and archers below deck, but be at the ready. If these be pirates they will not know us to have an armed force. We are fitted as a merchant ship." With Ethan's words the others moved below the deck, the archers set their bows and armed them at the ready. The ship approached quickly, coming along side the vessel carrying the party. From below deck Justin could hear Ethan call to the ship.

"What ho." No response came. "I say, what is your intent?" With this an answer could be heard from the vessel.

"Lower your sail and prepare to be boarded by the crew of Russel Strongbrow." The sound of clashing sabers could be heard even from below deck.

This was all that Justin's archers needed. If they could hear the sabers, they could hit the targets. Aaron and his fifteen archers mounted the deck and sent off a volley of arrows before the pirates knew what was coming towards them. Ten of the pirates were hit with the first array of arrows from the bows of Aaron's men. Aaron called for a second volley as the pirate captain sounded an alert. As the second flight of arrows sailed towards the ship the pirates found cover and started to arm themselves for a long range assault. Over the next few minutes the skilled archers of Balmoria exchanged arrows with the less proficient bowmen on the pirate ship, injuring many and killing a few of the buccaneers. The battle waged on.

The end of the battle came when Aaron managed to hit the well protected pirate captain, piercing him through the chest. As the bold marauder slumped to the deck of the vessel, his crew became panicked and confused. The remaining crew turned the ship sharply from Ethan's vessel for a moment, allowing Ethan and his crew the few precious seconds needed to catch the prevailing wind and sail free of the onslaught. The sounds of yells and screams of the pirate crew fell behind the ship of Balmoria, and the pirates were not seen again for the remainder of the trip.

***

After another uneventful day of sailing the western shore of the sea was spotted on the horizon and Ethan commanded the crew to turn north. At the end of the fifth day Justin was watching the shoreline for any sign of a harbour to be used. The lookout on the mast was the first to sight the long awaited coastal inlet.

"Straight ahead, sir, the coastline opens into a narrow harbour near the grey mountain. And look, to the northwest there can be seen the top of the tallest of the mountains, covered with white." The ship took to the bay as the sun finished its setting. After weighing the anchor, Ethan turned to Justin.

"We should stay aboard ship for the night, mounting a watch. We have no time to set a camp before night fall, and I do not know the area well enough to set a camp in the dark."

"Agreed. At first light we set to shore to set a camp. We shall take our leave from there." Justin ordered the army to stand down. Ethan did likewise with the sailors.

The group slept well that night to the gentle rocking of the cove waters. Justin, however, sat up late into the night staring at the mountain peak visible, white, on the skyline. By his feet lay the company of his followers, sighing deeply. Justin could not sleep for wondering what lay ahead, on the peak of the lonely mountain to the northwest.

7
Mountain Journey

The morning sun woke the tired party from their weary slumber. To Justin's amazement Sally could be found nowhere on the ship. As a the party was landing in the small ship's boat, a rustling in the underbrush brought every sword and bow to the ready. From the bushes stepped Sally, a large threaded sack dragging behind her.

"I am very sorry, but I am more of a night spider. I thought that while you slept I would do some hunting, here is a boar for our evening meal. Please be careful when you walk around to the far southern end of the beach. I have set my web on a well used path there." Justin greeted the misplaced spider warmly. The crew of the ship, hungered for anything but ships rations of hardtack and water, quickly set about the task of preparing the animal and a spit to roast it on so that it could cook through the day.

Sally showed three of the sailors where the web was so that they could gather provisions in the future, while the other members of the party set about erecting a camp on the beach site. All were refreshed by the smell of fresh meat starting to cook for their first meal on land. Justin called his commanders together for a brief assembly.

"We will spend today gathering provisions and preparing for our inland journey. As well, we will set camp on the beach for the sailors so that they can restock our shipboard supplies in our absence. Are there any other ideas of what we must do before we start our assault on the mountain tomorrow?"

"None other than the fact that we may want a small group to scout around this area to find the best advance for us to use come tomorrow." Aaron spoke freely, as if he had always been in the King's confidence. Justin admired this quality.

"Yes, very good. You, I, Lynette and Megan shall take a short tour around our immediate area. Ethan I will leave the troops, rats and Sally in your charge to set the camp for us all. Agreed?" A nod from the assembled team acknowledged their acceptance of the plan. "Good, then we shall set out within the hour."

***

The group of four searched the northwest end of the camp, where the path was recorded to lie in the journal, in sweeping half circles starting at the beach and moving progressively outwards from the shore. The branches overhead shielded them from the sun as they trudged through the jungle, yet the heat was only just to the point of being bearable. The sun was half way through its descent before they came across the sign they were looking for among a rock wall they were following through the woods.

"How about this?" Aaron called to the other three searchers. "The trees are thick, but the rock line is broken at this spot so that we can go through." Justin walked steadily to the spot.

"Cut away the branches and we shall take a look." Lynette and Aaron took their swords and removed several branches from the tree in quick order. "What lies ahead is in rough repair, but it is definitely a path. Let us proceed up a way and see if there are any other signs that this is the path we seek." With this Justin also took his sword and joined the two at cutting their way through the thick underbrush and branches that crossed the path more thickly that Sally's web.

The three cut their way along the overgrown pathway, Aaron at the ready with his bow, for more than an hour. After this the path opened into a small clearing in the forest. At the end of the clearing was the continuation of the trail they had just cut their way down. In front of this trail stood a large boulder sized stone. The group hurried to it. Carved into the top surface, weather beaten and almost unrecognizable, was the seal of Balmorain. The symbol left behind by Jacobis when he had followed the path confirmed what they had believed. This was what they were searching for.

***

They ate well that night. The boar meat was a welcomed change from the rations at sea. The army and crew feasted and danced late into the night to the music of a pipe and a violin. Justin stood alone at the north end of the camp, off from the feasting revelry of his party, gazing longingly at the white capped mountain. His mind wandered as he imagined what trials and hardships lay on the path ahead.

"Justin, are you well? You appear troubled." Justin gave a start as he turned to meet the eyes of Lynette. She had come upon the unsuspecting Justin as he stood, pondering.

"I am well, my friend. I was just lost in my own thoughts, that is all. How are the troops?" He motioned to the crowd of men and women farther down the beach.

"They sing too loud and drink too much, but they will be fine and ready by morning. What think you of our course tomorrow? How will our passage fare?"

"I would rather sleep in an Ice Wyrm bed, than escort us on the route we must take come sun rise.

However, I know the troops that accompany us are the finest we could have, the animals are strong, brave and loyal, and our future magician has more knowledge of my craft than I did at her age. Given a choice I would not go, but since I must I do not think we could have assembled a better team to pursue this quest. I worry, however, for the two small twins in our party."

"Robert and Michael? There is no need to worry for their sake. They may be small in stature, but they are tall in strength. None can pull the bow, or aim the arrow, better than they." She smiled at the fatigued monarch. "Their parents were foresters, and as such were skilled in the use of the bow. Robert and Michael have been using the bow since before they could walk. Sadly, their parents were frozen in the first Ice Wyrm attacks on the town while trying to hold the beasts away from attacking a mother and her four small children. They died soon after from their wounds. They were a close family. Michael and Robert, having a deep reverence for their parents as well as Balmoria, joined the army at the first call on your return. They shall be all right."

"Even so, I wish I knew what misery may wait for us on yonder mountain top." He turned to face the mountain once again.

"Whatever the adversity we shall face it together, Justin, and survive to see other days together." She placed a friendly hand on his arm. He took her hand and held it tightly in his. This touch was enough to draw his attention away from the mountain. The tumultuous uproar of the party filled the night air with song. They walked back down the beach in silence.

***

Early the next morning found the group in the clearing, which held the great rock. Justin inspected the huge boulder for any signs it may hold that may help them in their trip to come. All that he found carved on the rock, below the Seal of Balmorain, were the words 'Stay true to the straight and pure path, all who enter this quest, lest you die.'

"Comforting words, these. Makes me want to come back often." Aaron spoke with a slight quiver in his voice, but his words broke some tension, which the carving had built.

"Yes, let us proceed with care." Justin motioned towards the pathway to the north end of the clearing. "Sally if you could scout ahead it would be appreciated. Lynette and Aaron, half of your troop each before and after. Matthew and Mortimer at the lead. Megan and I will be together in the center of the group. Let us go."

With this the group split up as commanded and set off down the trail. The way was rough and the forest had mostly covered the pathway. The soldiers in front had to take it in turns to clear the overhanging branches as they walked. The trip was slow. Around mid day the group stopped to eat from the small portions, which they carried.

"Lynette, how far do you think we will need to walk to get to the top of the mountain?" Justin ate some of the cold pork as they spoke.

"From the height, assuming that we do not meet with much more resistance than we have been, we may be at the top in the span of three days. The path is not wider than would hold four abreast. We shall need to keep to this pace if we are to return in time to save Balmoria." They finished a hurried meal and set off again.

***

As night set in they came to a clearing in the path. They started to set camp for the night. Justin called together the party around the small fire they set to heat their meal.

"I fear that we cannot continue in the dark, for the path is covered with underbrush and will be hard to find with only torch light to guide us. Sally, what of the road ahead?"

"I have seen ahead for half a days march. The trees are thick, but the way is straight. We shall have no problems for the morning." Sally gave her report to the company.

"Very good, Sally, but we still must beware. The path, which we follow, is set with dangers. I have been given clues in the journal of my great ancestor, Jacobis of Balmorain, about the trail, which we now take. But they are only clues. He did not reveal the total of our journey, only alluding to the collection of trials, which we will face on the way. His only clear message was that we shall start at the rock with the shield of Balmorain. Of this space he wrote 'Follow not the lights of the night, but sleep well at the first opening of the path.' I do not know what this could mean, for to follow the lights of the night we should have to see them in the sky. All would be wise, though, to keep these words in mind." Justin sat on a log by the fire.

For hours the group just sat and talked about less frightening things than their journey. After the third hour one of the twins rose from the fire and stood staring into the forest. He silently started to walk towards an object that was obviously in his far off vision. Aaron stopped him with a word.

"Michael, where do you go?" He called after the brother.

"How do you know which is which? They are identical in all things." Justin interrupted with this query of the archer commander.

"Until our last battle I could not, my Lord. However, during that battle Michael was hit by a thrown rock and now has a scar on his forehead. Were it not for this I should not know one from the other." He turned back to the soldier who had taken yet more steps towards the forest edge.

"I say, Michael, where are you going?" Aaron stood up to approach the man who stood no taller than his own shoulder. He placed a hand on his arm.

"I am following the lights to see where they come from, can you not hear the call." The voice was dead, as if from a deep sleep. Aaron looked in the direction that Michael had been gazing, and soon he too stood fixed on the light. The two men stood motionless for a moment, then started to walk simultaneously towards the forest edge.

"Stop them, quickly." Lynette called to two infantry, who stood near by. The soldiers complied instantly, taking the two men by the arms and turning them around to face the fire. Life returned to their faces.

"The lights you have seen are Will-o-the-wisps. They are spirit creatures that dwell in the woods and lure people like yourselves to their deaths in the swamps and marshes of the forests. If you had followed them you would never have returned."

"I surmise that these are the lights of the night which Jacobis referred to. We must not look at them if we are to remain here. No one is to look into the forest when awake, for fear that we shall lose any able body." All the assembly nodded. Of all present Michael and Aaron agreed the most enthusiastically.

***

When they awoke they had lost one of their number, a soldier in Lynette's troop. She had awaken during the night, judging by the placement of her sleeping roll, and wandered into the forest. All agreed that the only explanation was the lights that Michael and Aaron had seen the night before. The party ate and then started their journey in silence. The realization came that they were far from untouchable.

They continued their upward trek along the unswerving path that lead to that for which they sought. As they traveled their spirits started to lift, the trees became less dense, and the air seemed to lose the heavy feeling it had in the thick of the forest. Around midday they came to a small clearing in the woods where they stopped for their small meal.

"The sun shining through the trees almost gives the forest here a glow, does it not?" Megan uttered as they sat amid the tall and spacious trees.

"Yes, it does. Almost a place where one would think to find Fairies." Aaron commented as he looked around.

"Aaron, you do not really believe that, do you?" Lynette laughed in disbelief.

"Certainly, one of the shipmen even described to me a time when she encountered a band of Fairies. Her party wandered too far into a forest when they were careening their boat. They fought something awful when startled." Aaron stated mater of factly.

"Well, I will not believe it unless I see some for myself." Lynette returned to her meal, chuckling to herself.

As if to fulfill her wish five human shapes flew through the air, one taking the morsel out of her hand as it passed. The small winged creatures dove at Lynette, causing her to drop to the ground. In a flash they were gone.

"Ha. Now I think you believe in Fairies, commander." Aaron spoke smugly.

"Come, all of you. It certainly looks like we are the interest of a scout party of Fairies, and I do not wish to try their friendly nature too much by remaining a long time. The book spoke nothing of the Fairies so I think they might be a recent addition to the area." Justin rose to his feet as he spoke. "We must leave at once."

With this the group picked up their belongings and started once again along the path ahead of them. More than one sword was at the ready, and many heads turned constantly to spy any movement in the trees. Justin turned to the wary Lynette.

"I hope the creatures did not frighten you too much, dear heart. They did no harm other than to your warrior ego." She chuckled and returned her unsheathed sword to its scabbard.

"I only wish that they did not answer my request so abruptly." A smile came to her mouth. "That is the last time, though, that I will refuse to believe in anything." She turned to Aaron and the two exchanged smiles.

***

The afternoon crept by without incident. Many times as they walked along the path, some of the company turned quickly to the surrounding forest to catch a full view of what they had seen from the corner of their eyes, but whatever they had seen was gone. There was little doubt that the

Fairies were following them, although their purpose was uncertain.

As night fell upon them they came to another clearing and set camp for the night. As the shadows grew in the light of the flickering fire, Justin told of the trials to come.

"The book did not tell much about the journey, apart from that which I have already shared with you, but it did tell about the end. Tomorrow we will come to a cavern at the top of the mountain. This cave will be guarded by a sentry. According to the book nothing shall help us at this passage." Justin stopped for a moment. "I only hope we can overcome this sentry even with no help."

"Shall we mount a guard tonight?" Aaron queried, "Even if just to watch for any attacks by the fairies, we still do not know their intentions."

"I think that you speak wisely, Aaron." Justin turned to Lynette. "They may be friendly, yet they may not."

"This is true." Lynette agreed. "I will mount a guard with both archers and infantry, on a rotating watch, throughout the night. Come morning we will need to all be as rested as possible." With this Justin started to retire as the two commanders divided their soldiers for the watches.

Just as the watches were set and the remainder joined their king for a long nights rest, the trees echoed with shrieks and yells. Justin leapt to his feet and stood where he had lain, staring frantically into the darkness of the forest for any creature, which had made the noise. From nowhere a small arrow shot out and pierced Justin's arm. He called in pain. The others turned to their leader. Justin pulled the small arrow from his arm and threw it to the ground.

"Just as I thought, the fairies are attacking us when we are most defenseless." Lynette called in the darkness. "Stoke up the fire and bring some light to our fight." Two soldiers instantly threw branches on the fire while the army searched the trees for their attackers. The flames blazed, lighting the surrounding darkness. In the new light the troops could see the creatures attacking them. They had four legs and wings, with the upper torso of a woman. Each carried a small bow and looked completely filthy and unpleasant. The archers were firing arrows at the airborne menace as Aaron called out.

"These are not fairies. These are harpies that I have heard tales of." Aaron barked orders to his archers between his explanations to Lynette, Justin and Megan. "But look, there are fairies amongst them, fighting as our allies."

What Aaron said was true, amongst the squadrons of harpies were the small humanoid forms of the fairies. The bands of winged creatures flew through the harpies troops, cutting them with their tiny swords. Although small, the spirit and agility of these wee warriors was the tonic that Justin's army needed to spur them on. Lynette, although distrustful of the fairies, could not help but agree with Aaron's judgment. She called to the legions of Balmoria.

"Ensure that you do not kill any of the Fairies. We seem to have camped in the domain of the Harpies tonight, and we can use any help that is supplied." She leapt from the clearing with her sword flashing in the light of the fire, her first stroke cutting a harpy in two.

The battle raged on for many hours. Fairies and humans fighting against the soiled, stinking body of harpies. Arrows and swords flashed in the night, as did the flame from Justin's Staff. In shock and frustration the harpies weaken after several hours and retreated to their lair in the forest.

The moon was at its highest in the night sky when the fight was ending, and the light was starting to die from the fire. The last harpies were routed from the clearing, and the dead bodies piled on the fire for disposal. None of the party were killed, but many were injured. Justin stood in the center of the clearing when a fairy drifted down and hovered in front of him.

"The harpies are dirty creatures, and the wounds you have sustained will be fowled with their excrement. Take this salve for your wounds, or else they will fester before they heal." Justin took the jar from the tiny hands of the fairy. Before he could respond the creature was gone.

"Thank you for your help. Thank you." As Justin called into the forest he walked to the edges of the clearing. He called over and over, "Thank you." When the silence of the woods promised that the last of the fairies had been seen, Justin turned back to the fire. He distributed the salve to all that were wounded. As he rubbed the cream onto his own shoulder all pain melted away in the coolness of the paste. Without another word, the party soon drifted off to sleep.

***

They woke early the following morning, still tired but ready to continue on their path. The warm morning air filled their lungs as they breathed deeply of the early mist. Knowing they were near the end of their journey spurred them steadily onwards. The bright sun of midday shone around them as they emerged from the woods. Ahead of them was a winding path reaching the top of the mountain summit. They stopped at the base before proceeding.

"We will stop to eat, then I will continue the journey. There is no reason for the rest to follow now." Justin addressed the group. Lynette answered.

"We have come to fulfill this journey with you. We would follow you even to the underworld. We shall follow you to the summit." The troops acknowledged their agreement.

"Then we shall set out after our refreshment." Justin took what little food remained from his pack.

They ate in silence, uncertain of what lay ahead. The sentry waiting for them frightened some, worried others, yet they all anxiously awaited the sight. Justin ate uncertainly, wondering what their challenger would resemble. After the meal they followed the twisted path before them.

As the sun was starting to set in the sky they reached the top of the climb. Mounting the pinnacle of the mountain they could clearly see the cave they had come so far to behold. Sitting at the mouth of the cave, on a chair made of rock, was a small child. The party gazed in wonder.

"He could not stop an insect should one try to enter." Aaron uttered in astonishment. "I cannot believe that Jacobis would warn against such an infant as this." He walked towards the child.

"Do not come farther, brave sir, least you be harmed in your effort to do good. Only the most worthy King may enter here." The child spoke in the voice of one advanced in age.

"Take care, Aaron, for everything is not always as it seems." Lynette warned the archer as he advanced.

"I am not afraid of such a small child, even if it does speak like my Grandfather." Aaron walked steadily forward.

When he was within two armlengths of the child, ready to reach out and grab it, a burst of light shot out from the youngster's eyes. Aaron was thrown ten lengths back from where he stood and landed with a thud on the ground. His moans witnessed that he was still alive.

"I did warn him of the danger. Only the true King, pure of deed, may enter here. You Justin, for I know your name, must enter to retrieve the stone. Though first you must answer this question, or you shall not see that which will save your Kingdom. Are you ready to hear the riddle?" The toddler smiled sweetly at the King and his party. Aaron rose from the ground and dusted off his clothing. Justin stood examining the child before him. He remembered the line from Jacobis' journal, which described this event. 'Nothing shall help you at this passage.' He felt little comfort from this advice.

"I will hear the riddle, young sir, but what are the consequences if I should fail." Justin stood some five lengths from the small human form.

"Then the same fire which threw your commander will destroy you. This is the first trial to obtain the stone. Do you still wish to continue?" The tiny face smiled the most angelic smile that Justin had ever seen. The guardian of this treasure was almost more that he could bear.

"I am prepared to continue." Justin stood firm at the entrance to the cave knowing that the army behind him would be no help should he fail.

8
The Cavern

The small boy smiled as he sat on his stone seat at the mouth of the cave. He gazed intently at Justin as he thought. Then he spoke.

"The riddle you must solve, to continue on your quest for the stone, is this. What is greater than God, more evil than a demon, the poor have it, the rich need it, and if you eat it you will die? Solve this problem and you may enter the cavern to seek your treasure." The child laughed as he rocked in his seat.

"May I have help with the problem?" Justin queried the boy.

"Yes you may, but only you may answer. And you will profit or perish from that answer. So answer wisely." Justin called together his small team of advisors.

"Are there any suggestions to the answer, friends?" Justin surveyed the puzzled faces, one at a time, and could tell that there was no ready answer in their minds.

"I can think of nothing, my Lord, which answers all of these things." Aaron answered, puzzled.

"Neither can I, Justin, though I feel that the answer should be right before my thoughts. The question is harder to answer than it should be." Lynette also stood in puzzlement.

"I wish I could help, by a spider's mind is unused to puzzles of this sort." As Sally spoke, Matthew and Mortimer nodded their agreement with her statement.

"Then we have come this far for nothing, for I cannot think of the answer either." Justin sighed with dejection. Megan spoke next.

"What is it that Jacobis said about this trial. Maybe we can think on this clue again."

"But it was not a clue. He said that nothing would help us." Justin tried to find any clue in this.

"Yes, but what did he write, exactly?" Justin thought hard to remember the words used on the paper in the journal.

"His words were 'nothing shall help you at this passage.' I still do not see how this will help us." Justin thought hard about the passage he remembered from the book.

"I think that is it. Nothing shall help us. Justin what is greater than God?" Megan asked in excitement.

"Why, nothing I suppose." Justin still did not understand the answer.

"And nothing is more evil than a demon, correct?" Megan prodded.

"Yes, that is true. Also the poor have nothing, and the rich need nothing." Lynette was excited by this revelation.

"And if you eat nothing you will die." Sally chimed in. Justin turned towards the cave and addressed the child sitting on the stone chair.

"Nothing." Justin walked towards the boy. "Our answer is nothing. This is the answer I give to your riddle, shall I enter or shall I die?" Justin stood firmly on the ground in front of the toddler.

As he stood an invisible curtain at the mouth of the cavern could be seen moving away, with sparkles and shimmers of light, clearing the entrance for Justin. The child jumped from his chair and clapped his hands.

"Correct. You have done well, good King. Now you must face the final test of your worth. Come forward to the mouth of the cave. Only you may go, as well as your young apprentice, for only a sorcerer may enter this magical cave and undergo the test." Megan joined Justin in front of the cave entrance. Justin took her hand in his.

"You do not have to go with me, sister." He smiled into her deep blue eyes.

"I know I do not, but I wish to. If I may be any help to you within, it would be better to risk death than to wait and do nothing." She smiled, her face brightening the already clear day. The two turned to the young boy.

"And what is this test which we must face?" Justin stood firm to his spot.

"In the cave you will find stairs leading down. Only those who's mission is pure will pass the stairs unharmed. At the base of these stairs you will find an oaken door, behind which lies a room containing two additional doors at the far end. In front of the two doors stand two guards. One always tells the truth, and the other always lies. You may ask one question, only, of one of the guards. Then you must choose a door. One contains the treasure, which you seek, the other contains death. You shall have no second choice." The child smiled with an angelic face throughout his telling of this horror. "Enter when you are willing." He turned from the King and his sister. Justin faced Lynette.

"Wish me luck." He smiled as he spoke. She returned his smile, not speaking. Justin took her hand in his and squeezed it tightly. Lynette leaned forward and kissed him softly. Justin returned the kiss from his childhood friend and companion. When she had pulled away, a little embarrassed, Justin smiled and nodded then turned to the cave. Justin and Megan walked steadily forward and into the mouth of the cave.

***

At the rear of the cavern they found the promised staircase, carved from the very rock of the mountain, leading down. They carefully descended the staircase, always watching for a trap or pitfall as they went. The darkness of the cave closed around them as they descended further and further into the earth until they could see nothing and had to feel to find their footsteps. When the hall was at its darkest, and their eyes became accustomed to the absence of light, they could see a sliver of light below them. This could only be from around the door for which they ventured.

As they stopped before the great door, searching for a handle with which to open it, the door swung away from them of its own accord. Stepping past the door, Justin and Megan saw a great room lit by dozens of torches secured to the walls. The cavernous room, nearly as big as the feast hall of Balmoria, glowed from the torch light as if it contained five thousand tiny suns affixed to the walls. The cavern was carved out of the rock of the mountain, and as such the walls were covered with thousands of gems of differing colours, both small and large, all reflecting and enhancing the light from the flares on the walls. The room was warm and bright, nothing like what Justin had expected in the centre of the ground. The two siblings stared at the rich beauty of the jewels, almost forgetting their quest, until their eyes came to the end of the large room. At the end were two massive doors of solid gold, glittering in the light.

Standing in front of the golden doors were two of the most beautiful nymphs Justin had ever seen or imagined.

Both were identical with long, flowing, blond hair and flawless complexions. Justin almost thought that nothing about these creatures could harm him, then he remembered Aaron's flight when he tried to enter the cave. Nothing here was as it seemed.

"Welcome, Justin, and welcome to your sister and apprentice, Megan." The two spoke as one in a quiet, almost musical, tone. "What question do you have?" Justin had not thought about the question he would ask when he stood in the great room.

"I must first gain council from my apprentice before I ask my question." Justin spoke to the two in turn, careful not to ask a question.

"But of course, for both of you are in peril should your choice be wrong." Once again the lilting tones of the voices did not match the terror of their threat. Justin turned to Megan and spoke quietly.

"Have you any thoughts on what question we should ask which will give us an unerring clue to the identity of the truthful Nymph?"

"Even if we can figure which is the truthful Nymph we shall still not know which door to choose, for we can ask only one question. We need a question which will tell us the door to choose even if we ask the wrong Nymph." Megan sat puzzled for several minutes, thinking. "Did Jacobis not also give clues to this trial.

"Only one. He said, 'Ask one of the other then listen not.' This made little sense to me when I read the passage, and even less now." Justin thought along with his sister for a long while. Time passed slowly as the two sat motionless, thinking without a word. "Wait, I have a thought. 'Ask one of the other', this must mean to ask one nymph about the other one, since we cannot be sure of receiving a straight answer to our question. We must ask an indirect one."

"Yes, and that one must speak for the other. If we query the truthful Nymph of what the other would say she must tell a lie. And if we query the untruthful Nymph of what the other would say she must also tell a lie." Megan could almost grasp the idea, but not fully.

"That is it. If asked what the other would tell us then both would tell us a lie, as they must. So if we ask what the other would say is the door to the treasure, we would be told the door to death." Justin smiled.

"Then we would pick the other door. As Jacobis said, we would not listen to them. Yes, Justin, this is it." She jumped to her feet. "Quickly, ask either the question so that we may return in time." Justin approached the Nymph in front of the right hand door.

"If I should ask that Nymph what door held the stone for which I seek, which door would she tell me it lay behind?" Justin awaited the answer for what seemed like hours.

"She would tell you that it lies behind this door which is behind me." The Nymph smiled as she answered.

"Thank you for your answer, and for your help." Justin walked slowly to the door on the left of the great room. "I choose this door to be opened." The Nymph stepped aside to let Justin turn the handle on the door. As the great metal slab pulled away from the wall, no demons of death screamed out at them. The door opened to reveal a small room lit with torches. In the center was a lidded box carved from the very rock of the floor. The stone must lie within.

***

Justin hurried to the box at the center of the room. He placed his hands on the lid of the box and caressed it. Contained in this box was the stone that would save Balmoria from the clutches of the evil Deirdre. Carved in the top of the box was the seal of Jacobis of Balmorain. Justin knew that this was the moment he had waited for since starting his journey. He gripped the corners of the lid and slowly lifted the top.

It slid back and away from the box easily with his touch. The loaf sized stone shone with a dark, black light within. Justin could feel and sense the evil. It was both cold and warm to the touch. Cold from the evil it contained, yet warm with the invitation to power. He lifted the rock from its resting place in the box and slipped it into the satchel under his cloak. He rose and turned to see Megan standing in the doorway smiling. Behind her were the two Nymphs. One spoke, however which was the truthful Nymph had been lost to Justin.

"You must hurry your journey to Balmoria, I am afraid. Your help is gravely needed there." Whether the Nymph spoke truly or no, she was correct in one fact, the quest for the stone was over. Now the difficulty, and the urgency, was to return to Balmoria before it was too late.

***

Justin hurried quickly from the room in the cave and started up the stairs, the heavy stone slowing his progress. Megan rushed behind him. They stepped from the cavern into the early light of the rising sun. Lynette, standing worried where she had been when the two siblings had entered the cave, let out a cry of joy and raced towards them.

"Justin, I was worried that you would not return, you were gone for more than twelve hours. I tried to follow but that evil whelp had once again closed the magical door to the cave. Are you injured at all?" Lynette could not hold back her emotions.

"We are fine. I did not realize that it had been so long. Time must stand still for any that are in the cave. We have the stone, and we must get it back to Balmoria before time has run out for our fair country." Justin once again called the council of commanders together.

"We must leave immediately and lose no further time. The stone must be returned to Balmoria quickly." They broke camp quickly, then started for the bottom of the mountain path.

At the base of the mountain they entered the forest path they had emerged from over half a day before. It seemed so long since then that they could hardly imagine what it had felt like to be in the forest, but the way was clear and the path lead downwards. The weight of the stone slowed Justin only slightly. By midday they were at the clearing where the Harpies had attacked them only two nights before. The downward slope, and the urgency of their journey, sped their progress. After a hurried meal they were once again off on their trek. They came to the small clearing where they had dined for their noon meal and met the Fairies. Justin called the group together.

"We have come to a decision that I do not want to make alone. Do we stop here for the night, or do we set torches and continue on?" He surveyed the group around him.

"I for one would like to continue." Megan spoke with a clear, authoritative voice. "We have come this far in the light, and can be at the entrance come morning if we march through the night. The path is cleared of trees from our ascent, so we will not have to worry so much about getting lost as when we came up this trail. We will not have to worry about night dangers like the Will-o-the-wisps or the Harpies if we do not stop, and we will be able to sleep when we reach the ship. We can be at the ship by mid morning since we are traveling downhill, and we must waste as little time as we can."

"Wisely said, I think we should continue." Lynette looked to the remainder of the group.

"I am in agreement also." Aaron turned to the three animals. "Is it settled then?"

"Yes, we agree to continue also." Sally spoke as the two mice nodded.

"We will find torches then and continue on our way." Justin spoke with finality. "I hope we will be at the ship in time to sail before noon. The sooner we return, the sooner we can use the stone we have laboured so long to attain."

"How does the stone weigh you down? Do you need assistance to carry it?" Lynette asked with concern.

"I will manage. Let us continue." This said, the party assembled torches from the felled branches of their ascent and continued down the path.

***

The night was dark and silent, save for the moaning and creaking of the trees around them. The flaring branches lit the path ahead and to the rear. The group continued on past the clearing of the Will-o-the-wisps. After the sun had mounted its steed for the ride across the sky, and the torches were extinguished in the dim light of the morning, the troop stopped for a hasty meal to replenish their strength and renew their vigor.

"We are but a mornings walk from the end of our path, and then only an hour to the ship. I only hope that Ethan has the ship prepared to sail on our arrival." Justin took the last drink of water from his depleted water skin. "Our arrival could not have come at a better time, my water bladder is in need of refilling."

"As is our store of food. We could not have timed this journey better in the way of food and drink. I hope the ship's crew have been able to restock our stores in the last days." Aaron took the last bite of his meal.

"Come, we must head on before our weariness overtakes us and we cannot continue." As Justin called the troop rose to their feet and prepared to march. At the head of the line were the two brothers. Justin shook his head in astonishment. "How two such slender and frail bodies can hold such stamina and strength is beyond my reasoning."

"They are certainly a wonder, and an advantage, on this voyage." Aaron proceeded to rally the troops for the final leg of their descent.

***

Justin and his contingent appeared on the beach just as the sun was starting to descend the sky. They found Ethan and his men packed and ready for the journey. They rowed to the ship on the oar boats and climbed aboard. There to greet them was their captain.

"Welcome back aboard, I trust you have found the stone?" Ethan proceeded to help the crew prepare to sail.

"How did you know we were to arrive now? It is as if you had just packed everything away this morning." Justin mounted the gunwales of the boat.

"We could see your torches in the night as you descended the mountain. We judged that you would be here by midday so we struck camp, cut the spider's nets, and prepared to sail. The stay over gave us the opportunity to careen the vessel and remove the barnacles on her hull. Any more time and we should have need of more to do." Ethan smiled as the ship pulled out from the cove and into the open sea.

"My thanks on your preparedness. We need to make haste to return to Balmoria."

"With the wind at our back, and with any luck, we shall be there in less time than we came, having sailed against the wind the whole journey here." The sails billowed with the easterly wind and the ship sped on its way.

The crew set to work on the sails, happy to be once again toiling on the rigging. The army lay sleeping on the deck, tired from their journey down the mountain. Ethan called Justin below deck at mid morning. The storeroom was filled to the last space with all manner of food.

"During your absence we have caught and smoked more boars, fish and some sea birds for all when we return. Also we have found and collected the fruits of ten different trees, which were growing near the shoreline. This should help all of Balmoria on our return." Justin surveyed the piles of food as the captain spoke.

"You have done well my friend. I only hope there remain some to eat this bounty of food on our return. I fear that things may not have gone well with our comrades in the castle."

"I only hope that you are wrong in your fear." Ethan closed the stores and preceded Justin onto the deck.

Justin's weary eyes closed soon after he lay his head on the deck beside the sleeping form of Lynette.

***

Justin awoke before the others to the smell of salt air and the sound of the wind in the sails. He rose from the deck and leant a hand to the sailors on deck. The unaccustomed work enlivened his spirits.

"Did you sleep well, my King?" A dusty and weather beaten sailor hauled on a rope beside the young sorcerer.

"Yes I did, the rest has done me good." They pulled as the sail adjusted into its place.

"We shall get to Balmoria soon, you shall see." They finished the task and went about the business of sailing the ship. Justin thought only of Balmoria and the task still ahead on their return home.

Two days passed on the sea. The cove and shore of the land was far from sight behind them, and the coast of Balmoria far ahead and out of sight in front. On the horizon, closing fast, were the billowing sails of another ship.

"What are the sails on the horizon?" Lynette queried the captain.

"They appear to be the same ship which attacked us on the first leg of our journey. We must drop our flag and hope that they do not recognize us. For if they do then they will know our strengths and may counter them." Thus said the flag was lowered from the mast. The ship came closer to the sloop as the army crouched down on the deck of the ship. Time passed slowly as the two ships approached each other. After an hour noise could be heard from the other ship. It was indeed the pirates. Ethan waited for them to call first.

"Surrender, to the pirates of Russel Strongbrow. And then your lives might be spared for to join our number." The pirates called and yelled in response to their leader's cries.

"I see they have bandaged some of their wounds since our last encounter." Ethan spoke quietly to the army on the deck. "Shall we see if they can still remember our archers?"

With this the archers, their bows at the ready, stood and fired at the pirate vessel. As the arrows flew through the air, the pirates each raised a shield before them to stop the projectiles. After the first volley the pirates lowered their shields and laughed.

"Did you not think we recognized you from before. Your arrows will do not harm to us now. Surrender your ship and her cargo." The pirates laughed as their ship closed the gap between the two sea vessels. Ethan did not know what to do.

"Set your arrows aflame and fire into the rigging." Megan called to the archers. At this two of the remaining soldiers prepared and lit a pot with small kindling while others wrapped arrows in cloth. Within a minute cloth covered arrows were set alight and flames were sent aloft into the rigging of the attacking ship.

The pirates, not suspecting this maneuver, hurried in panic as the sail caught flames. A dozen men crawled into the rigging to extinguish the flaming sail. The others started to return fire on the ship with bows of their own. The skillfully shot arrows of Aaron's archers continued to hit their marks. Many of the sailors in the sails were knocked from their perch by a well placed arrow and plummeted to the sea below. As the fight raged on the flames on the pirate ship continued to grow and get out of hand. Soon the sail was half gone, and as more men were needed to fight the rising fire, fewer were available to man the bows and attack the ship. "Quickly, turn the ship from them. With their badly burnt sail and rigging they surely will not be able to follow as we pull away."

As the sailors of Balmoria steered the ship away from the pirate vessel, the archers continued their onslaught against the brigand gang. As the buccaneers hurried to extinguish their vessel the sailors of Ethan's command widened the gap between the two vessels. As the pirate ship started to fall from sight the flames could still be seen in the distance. The group of Balmoria gave a cheer. Curses could be heard across the water.

***

Favourable winds, and fine sailing, brought the ship in sight of the Balmoria harbour in short of five days. The witch must have lowered her guard for she did not hinder their advance in any way. The ship raced across the open water separating them from the shore. The dock was all but deserted as they landed the craft and tied up from their journey. Waiting for them were Rebekah, Arthur, Malcolm and Shanawn along with Jason and Katarina. The battle weary faces spoke more than Justin wanted to know.

"Call the troops. Ethan and his crew have stored a good quantity of food for us as they waited for our return. We will meet within the hour for an update on our position in this battle. May we hold for yet one last battle. I have the stone." With this he smiled wearily to the assembly, turned towards the beaten castle, and preceded the group towards it.

9
The Final Battle

The stores had been packed into the castle and the commanders had gathered in the battle room to plan the next phase of the war. Justin, concerned for the many vacant chairs, prompted his aunt to speak of the events of the fortnight he had been away.

"When the witch determined that you had gone, she once again sent the mice against the castle. Her army had grown since the last attack and the new troops were not yet ready for battle. In the first battle, some seven days from your departure, the infantry units took the lead of the battle since the mice were attacking in the hills to the north. Jason's infantry was destroyed to a dozen men. Katarina, in control of Brandalon's force, lost some ten soldiers. Blaindoro's cavalry sustained damage of ten soldiers also.

"In the second attack, four days from the first onslaught, the cavalry was more in use. Blaindoro was felled in the battle from a thrown spear, as was Alaynia who had taken her archers to the base of the castle walls to increase their efficiency in battle. One rogue mouse, apart from his unit, descended on Alaynia in the heat of battle. Some fifteen archers were also lost in the battle, although they killed more enemies in this battle than they had in any other. Brandalon, who had taken from his bed without permission, armed himself and went into battle alone, not leading a troop. After a fierce hand to hand combat with the chief mouse warrior he cut deep into the heart of the animal and killed it, only to fall to the ground of his own wounds and be mauled by a swarm of rodents before any could come to his aid. In total, thirty infantry and twenty-five cavalry were killed in the battle. The remainder are weary and wounded, but prepared to battle for Balmoria." Rebekah stopped her tale and turned to Justin. He surveyed the anxious faces at the table before he spoke. Silently he took the rock from the satchel at his side and placed it on the table.

"This is our salvation. We must mount a direct offense against the witch's lair. When we are inside we must force her to hold the stone, then we must speak the words written on the stone itself. What are our numbers?" He turned to Malcolm.

"In total, with new recruits, ninety infantry under three commanders, fifty-seven cavalry and forty archers with no commander."

"Make that one commander for the archers, Aaron has proved himself worthy on our trip and will take the lead."

"Still a small force to tackle such a mighty goal. And no leader for the cavalry. I only hope luck is on our side." Malcolm stopped his hand motions and sat motionless.

"All will be on foot as we are going into the mountains and horses will be of no use there. The cavalry will be split amongst the infantry commanders. We shall prepare and start our attack at daybreak. Gather and arm any new recruits you can find. Is there any other information I need to know?" Justin held the stone firmly in his hands.

"Only one thing." Arthur spoke from his chair near the king. "We have found that if a small keg of the blackened powder is equipped with a small candle wick, it can be thrown against the crowd and cause a small explosion in their midst. This may be useful in our attack."

"Indeed it will. Jason, your infantry will be equipped with this weapon for use in the battle. Let us now retire to prepare." With this all rose and filed out of the room. Justin approached Arthur and Shanawn.

"I see you have also acquired sorcerer staves for our apprentices, could it be that they are also outfitted as my own is?" He asked of Arthur

"Yes, Shanawn and I made them in the first lull before the battles. We also modified my own staff. These may also come in handy, when we fight with you in the battle." He smiled a weary smile.

"I would say no, but I have not known you to listen to my commands before. Let us prepare for the fight." The small assembly of magicians separated from each other for the night.

***

The whole assembly gathered on the castle bailey, armed for battle, as the eastern horizon started to glow red with the beams of the rising sun. Megan and Shanawn had acquired two shirts of chain mail to fit them, and Arthur had donned his old plate mail vest that Justin had seen hanging in the corner of the magician's tower throughout his childhood. The troops were at the ready as Justin stepped into the open space and commanded the gathering.

"Come my friends. We shall put an end to Deirdre's power over us today, or we shall die trying. Either way we shall not see Balmoria under her spell again." The crowd let out a cheer of support for Justin and the army. "I see no way we can plan for this assault, my good Malcolm, for we do not know which way we go. But I see that you are ready to accompany us to give us your advice as it can be given." The two clasped arms. Rebekah said a blessing over the amassed army, asking the powers for their protection and safe return. Once she was finished the drawbridge was lowered and the troops marched over the wooden planks and turned towards the mountains of the north.

The columns marched in file across the hills and plains, which lead to the base of the mountain. At the base they stopped and stood, looking into the forbidding rocks, which rose above them. No one moved, and not a sound was heard except for the wind rustling through the sparse grasses, which covered the mountainside. For moments the mountain was still, and Justin thought that they may yet be unexpected. Then one mouse rose from behind a rock and screamed. Three hundred mice stood to the call of their commander, armed and ready to do battle, and ran screaming down the mountain towards the scarce troops of Balmoria.

"To the bow." Aaron called to the archers. All had drawn and shot before the last echo from his call had quieted. Over two dozen mice warriors were felled or wounded.

"Forward!" Lynette's call spurred the warriors forward to combat the mice, hand to hand. Two more volleys of arrows were fired before the infantry closed the distance between the archers and the mice, blocking clear volleys of arrows from the bows.

"We must now take our separate ways, friends. Stay to the back of the battle, aim true and strike when you have a clear opportunity, and take care for selves." Aaron called to the archers. "Half of you split to the left and the rest follow me to the right." With this the archers fanned out to the edges of the battle to lend what aid they could to the battling foot soldiers.

***

The infantry pushed an offense up the centre of the enemy warriors. Flanking to the right and left.

"Jason! Take your troops to the right. Katarina and I will take the harder route to the left. The mice and Sally are protecting Justin, the sorcerers and Malcolm." Lynette called to the commanders. "Last one to the Witch's cave buys the drinks after the battle."

"You forget. We have a secret weapon to clear the way." Jason jeered back. "One round of powder. Now." On command twenty small kegs of powder were lit and thrown forward into the midst of the unsuspecting mice. The explosions threw rocks, dirt and bodies into the air. Nearby mice turned to see what had happened, only to be overrun by the forces of Balmoria. Jason pushed his warriors forward into the fray. Swords crashed as the humans fought against the sturdy rodents, pushing ever upwards to their goal.

***

The mouse commander pushed his way forward through the line of humans and mice intertwined in battle, until he stood before Lynette. The two mighty warriors stood facing each other for moments which seemed to stretch into hours, oblivious to all that was happening around them, neither moving. Lynette stared into the inky blackness of the creatures eyes, staring deeply into his soul and finding nothing but black void. This creature of battle had no thought or feeling to hold him back. Created by the witch he could feel only courage, and fear.

She knew he could feel fear. He raised his sword and with a lunge forward he struck out against the human commander. Her training took over and she instinctively raised her shield to take the blow. Unsteady she was pushed three armlengths back down the mountain. Regaining her balance she used her momentum to counter his attack and swung her sword forward into his unprotected flank. The mouse pulled back to avoid contact with the blade, but came short. Blood trickled from the hand width cut in his side, just below his armour. The rodent had the advantage of strength, but Lynette had the advantage of skill and speed. The match was even.

Lynette fought bravely against the tall, strong adversary. For ten minutes they matched strength for agility, the mouse pushing Lynette down the mountainside with a mighty blow, then pulling back himself as her nimble blade shot out at his unprotected side. The combat continued for half of an hour until, with a mighty blow, the mouse shattered Lynette's sword and knocked her to the ground. She lay dazed on the earth where her head had struck a stone, staring once more up into the cold black eyes of this conjured warrior.

He towered over her for a moment, sword raised to strike into her heart. Suddenly an arrow flew through the air and struck the mouse in the chest, piercing his armour and knocking him backwards onto a boulder. Lynette leapt to her feet, her head spinning from where it had struck the stone, and snatched the beasts own sword from the ground where it had fallen. With one deft motion she lowered the blade sharply onto the rodents neck, killing it.

She turned to see one of the twins, bow raised, smiling. He gave her a salute of friendship, the turned back towards the battle. Lynette once again raised the large sword of the mouse commander and continued up the mountain.

***

Katarina's troops closed in on a stronghold of mice secured behind an outcrop of rocks. The warriors climbed over the top of the mound and came at the company of rodents from above, a tactic they had not expected. The group of twenty mice fought strongly against the onslaught of Katarina's troops, but they could not stand against the fierce attack of the small force. Katarina stood on the outcropping of rocks. To the south clouds formed, threatening to wash away the efforts of the tiny force.

"To the cave. Push ahead, soldiers. We shall stop Deirdre before the storm falls. Forward."

***

Justin and the team of sorcerers moved steadily up the rise, setting on fire any mice that ventured too close. Matthew and Mortimer, wearing vests emblazoned with the seal of Balmoria so that they would not be confused as the enemy, fought bravely to clear the way up the mountain for the group.

Sally, endowed as she was with eight arms, needed no weapon for the battle. In seconds she could disarm any mouse, hold him down, and spin her web around his body. In doing so she immobilized him from the battle, and her poison stopped any attempt to escape.

As the battle raged on the clouds continued to form to the south. The brewing storm threatened the hold the forces of Balmoria from scaling the mountain.

"We must move quickly." Justin called to Lynette and the commanders. "The storm to the south may well wash us from the mountain, then all will have been for nothing." The call went out to all troops, and the battle was fought even more fiercely than it had been fought before.

***

The troops pushed their way towards the summit, leaving bodies of both friend and foe in the path they trod. Within the hour they pushed the remaining mice to the entrance of the cave. With one crack of lightning and thunder the storm announced its arrival. The few mice started in fear and, dropping their weapons, turned and ran from the cave entrance into the mountains.

"Jason and Lynette, hunt down the remaining few. Katarina, guard our backs at the door. Matthew, Mortimer, Sally and the sorcerers will enter alone with me." With this the rains started to stream from the sky. Justin and his group, swords and staves drawn, entered the cave and strode down a long shaft into its heart. At the end of the long corridor a shaft of pale, flickering light beckoned to the small party. They stepped slowly and quietly along the smooth walled channel. At the end they turned a corner to see a large, scarcely lit chamber, the home of Deirdre.

***

Standing near a fire at the back of the cave, was a short creature dressed in a long, black, hooded cloak covering the entire body from head to foot. The cave was a small black opening in the earth, hardly a centre for conquering a kingdom. The thick black walls absorbed what little light was created by the small, smokey fire which filled the room with a stench that impaired the nose and burnt the lungs. Justin stepped forward into the cavern and stood gazing at the lone figure as the remaining people spread along the two walls on either side of him.

As the party stopped moving the humanoid form turned from the fire, threw her hood back, and looked directly into the eyes of Justin. Her face, for they could tell now that it was a woman, was neither old nor young. Small wrinkles accented her mouth and eyes. Her mouth twisted in a sinister sneer as she took a step towards the young sorcerer, staring through him as she walked. Although she did not look old, years of abuse, treachery, and trickery showed in every small line of her face.

"I knew you would come, though you cannot win." Justin took the stone from his bag and held it for her to see. "Do you think that you can make me touch the stone of power, sorcerer. You can hardly turn rock to water. Pathetic magician. Do you think you can defeat the power of Deirdre, mistress of the dark."

"We shall defeat you," with this Shanawn stepped forward and shot a fireball from her staff. With a wave of her hand Deirdre brushed it aside and sent it hurtling back at the young apprentice, who dropped back under the heat of the flame, and fell to the ground. Megan rushed to her aid.

"Worthless trickery. Is this how you insult my powers? No mortal man shall hold me to his laws, Justin, this you must know. And you are such a mortal man." With this Deirdre sent a visible bolt of power from her fingers, striking Justin and lifting him from the ground. Suspended in mid air, having dropped the stone, Justin could do nothing but scream. Deirdre cackled as she held him helplessly dangling in the air.

***

As Deirdre laughed the beam of power was cut to Justin. He fell to the floor. Deirdre screamed as the huge black form of Sally appeared out of nowhere, taking the full force of the beam. With her many hands she held the witch's arms, and forced them onto the stone she held. The witch kicked and shrieked as Sally held her limbs, one at a time, and forced them to do as she bid. Sally spoke sweetly like only a spider can.

"I am not such a man." She smiled, then began the incantation. "'Comme forthe frome thise creature, evile thate you be, and seale yourselfe unto thise boxe were you may do noe furthere harme'." Having spoken the words on the stone it glowed brightly with a black light, which filled the cavern.

Deirdre shrieked as the evil power was pulled from her body and encased in the stone. Then she fell unconscious on the floor. Sally too drooped at the completion of her task and slumped to the hard stone floor. Justin rushed to her side, and found that he could do nothing. As he watched, the life force ebbed from her tired body.

"Sally, most noble spider and truest friend, thank you for my life." Justin stood over her, tears flowing freely from his eyes.

"Do not cry for me, my handsome king. My year span was growing long and nearing its end. I would surely have died soon. It was better that I could help before my end, for I would not have wanted to end without the knowledge that you were safe." She smiled. "Fare well, sweet Justin. No greater a King shall reign over Balmoria, or my heart." With this spoken, her eyes shut and she breathed her last.

"Mortimer, take her body with you. We shall burn it as one deserving of a pyre. Matthew, bring Deirdre, we shall deal with her mischief later." With this he took the stone from the ground and returned it to the satchel. Turning to a grotto in the cave wall he saw a small plant, with a form like that of his brother in the courtyard, in a basin of green, foul smelling liquid. Around this plant was the chain bearing Peter's holy symbol. Justin took this amulet from the shrine and placed it in the folds of his cloak. He turned to see Shanawn and Megan standing beside Arthur, smiling wearily. He smiled back. The battle was over.

***

Justin and the group stepped from the mouth of the cave into the light of the clear afternoon sun. They were greeted by three commanders at the entrance.

"What of Jason?" The look in their eyes told him what he knew already. Lynette spoke with a firm, controlled voice.

"In the final battle the mice were pushed up the mountain, followed by the troops of Jason and myself. Above was a rogue band of Mice which joined with those retreating. In the fray that followed Jason was felled, but the mice were destroyed." Her face crumbled into tears.

"Deirdre's power has been drained. We will not be troubled more by her. He did not die in vain." Justin turned to see Michael standing off alone, bow in hand. He walked towards him and addressed the young archer. "Robert?"

"He lies dead, my lord, for the salvation of Balmoria." The young soldier bowed his head as tears rolled down his cheek. Arthur placed his hand on the youth's shoulder and spoke in the voice of wisdom.

"Although we have gained a victory today, we have lost many a friend. It is a sad day." The group bowed their heads in sorrow. The battle was ended, but the grief continued.

10
Sending

Justin led the small band of returning warriors to the castle. The two mice took Deirdre to a room and locked her in for her safety. Justin strode to the structure in the centre of the courtyard, tore open one side, then pulled the chain from the folds of his cloak. He placed it around the 'neck' of the plant and stepped away. As all watched the limbs of the plant moved, and changed, and transformed into the figure of Peter standing before them, his black hair blowing around his pale face. He embraced Justin in greeting.

"I believe that this belongs to you." Justin took the crown of the warrior king from his head and began to place it on the head of his brother. Peter snatched it from his hand.

"My dear brother, I no more deserve to wear this crown and reign over Balmoria, than I do to carry the staff of a sorcerer. During my enchantment, though I could not move or speak, I could hear and see. You have proven your strength and wisdom in ruling during this time of war, and have thus earned the right to wear the crown and rule as king through your baptism of fire. I was raised to the life of a cleric, and a cleric I shall remain." He raised his voice for all to hear. "I decline any rights I have to the crown of Balmoria, and leave them to my brother, Justin, to reign as king. Long live the King." As Peter placed the crown on Justin's head the crowd roared its approval. Justin embraced Peter once again.

***

The troops gathered the bodies of the dead from the battlefield and amassed them for the funeral Pyre. Sally placed separate from the others. As the flames leaped upwards Rebekah called to the people.

"Today we start to rebuild the grandeur of Balmoria. These have died to aid this cause, not by force but by their own free will. We should be glad that this day is here, for their sake, for without them this day would not be. We must rejoice in their sacrifice, and give glory to their deeds." The assembly cheered and sang for the fallen heroes. When the flames had died to embers, and the smoke rose no more, the entire population of Balmoria slowly and quietly returned to the castle.

***

Deirdre was brought before the council in the war room. She stood in defiance before the assembly. Justin spoke.

"Although your deeds were evil and wicked, it has been ensured that you can do no further harm. You may chose any direction that you wish and you shall have safe passage to the borders of Balmoria, for I fear that your life may not be safe within her domains. You shall be given food enough to sustain you for your journey, and clothing which will not denote you as a witch. May you be speeded on your way, and blessed in your life." With this she was led out of the room and escorted on her way.

"My remaining commanders, it is up to us to rebuild Balmoria from her toppled ruins. Aaron and Michael will split the Archers and be sent to hunt wild game in the Forest of Jacobis to the east. Katarina with the remaining infantry and cavalry units will help to rebuild the city. We shall make Balmoria great once again for our children and our children's children." Aaron spoke in reply.

"Your confidence in us is flattering, my lord, but I must ask. What of Lynette? She has served as we have and more."

"Lynette, has agreed to be my Queen. We were to announce this to the people later at a feast of celebration." The cheers from the room could be heard in the courtyard.

"This is wonderful news, my lord. No greater a Queen could you have found." Katarina spoke in congratulations.

"Now we must turn to our task. Thank you all in advance for your support." Justin dismissed the crowd of commanders from the room.

***

After several weeks the tattered remains of Balmoria were slowly pieced together. People returned to the homes they had loved before the terror came from the north. The main occupation for the troops was to help rebuild the structures of the nearly destroyed town.

Ethan and his crew, after dropping Deirdre at a port on the south shore of the sea, returned laden with a shipload of food sent from that kingdom. With the game hunted by the archers this was enough to store for the winter months and more.

Grass returned to the hills and valleys of the kingdom. Peter and Rebekah continued to help the people rebuild from their torn past. Malcolm assisted in any way he could. Matthew and Mortimer also strove hard to care for the people they had fought so hard to protect.

***

Justin and Lynette were married before the whole population of Balmoria, amidst a feast which lasted for three days. At the end of the great feast Arthur and Justin called aside the two young girls.

"The time has come when you must learn from others than ourselves." Justin spoke. "To the east lies a larger mountain than this, and at its base stands a building of learning. A building of Sorcerers. In this building you will be taught all you need to know about magic and the ways of working nature. After nine years you will return, our worthy apprentices. Show them these at the door and they will let you enter." With this he placed his owl amulet around the neck of Megan. Arthur did the same, placing his hawk amulet around Shanawn's neck.

The four sorcerer's embraced each other for a long time. Justin whispered into their ears. "Remember magic is five parts what you do and ninety-five parts what others think you did." The girls smiled knowingly, and would never forget.